The Adventures of

ALFIE ONION

Other books by Vivian French

The Most Wonderful Thing in the World

Tales from the Five Kingdoms:
The Robe of Skulls
The Bag of Bones
The Heart of Glass
The Flight of Dragons
The Music of Zombies
The Snarling of Wolves

The Adventures of
ALFIE ONION

VIVIAN FRENCH

illustrated by Marta Kissi

WALKER
BOOKS

First published 2016 by Walker Books Ltd
87 Vauxhall Walk, London SE11 5HJ

2 4 6 8 10 9 7 5 3 1

Text © 2016 Vivian French
Illustrations © 2016 Marta Kissi

The right of Vivian French and Marta Kissi
to be identified as author and illustrator respectively
of this work has been asserted by them in accordance
with the Copyright, Designs and Patents Act 1988

This book has been typeset in Berkeley Oldstyle Book

Printed and bound in Great Britain by Clays Ltd, St Ives plc

British Library Cataloguing in Publication Data:
a catalogue record for this book is available
from the British Library

ISBN 978-1-4063-6310-4

www.walker.co.uk

For my dear friends Nick and Jon, with love
V. F.

For James, with all my love
M.K.

Chapter One

LONG, LONG AGO, when trolls lurked in deep dark forests and ogres grumbled and mumbled beyond the distant hills, there was a small and ordinary village called Guttersbury. The villagers were ordinary too, and Aggie Lumpett, the only daughter of the road sweeper, was just as ordinary as anyone else … until her tenth birthday. On this particular birthday, Aggie's father gave her a book of fairy tales. By her eleventh birthday she knew every single one by heart, and by her twelfth she had decided what to do with her life. She was going to marry a prince and live happily ever after.

By her sixteenth birthday Aggie had realised this was unlikely to happen – princes did not come to Guttersbury looking for their brides. She gave up walking up and down the high street in her best white nightgown, read her stories all over again, and changed her plans. What she needed was a hero, a hero who would go adventuring and bring back everything necessary for Happily Ever After and Glorious Luxury. And, as she had seen no heroes wandering around Guttersbury in all her sixteen years, she would have to arrange this for herself. What she needed was the seventh son of a seventh son. The book said the seventh son of a seventh son was ALWAYS a hero; all Aggie had to do was find one.

Aggie Lumpett was a determined girl. She walked from village to village and farm to farm, and at last she found Garf Onion. Garf was the seventh son of a pig farmer and all he really cared about was pigs, but Aggie pursued him with such enthusiasm that they were married on her eighteenth birthday. They set up home in Pigsticking Farm, and many years later their seventh son finally arrived. Aggie was over the moon; at last she was the proud mother of the seventh son of a seventh son.

"He's going to be a hero," she announced, "so we're going to call him Magnifico." Garf Onion shrugged and went back to his pigs, leaving Aggie to begin the hero's training. She was mildly inconvenienced by the arrival of an eighth son a year later, but she put his cradle in the barn and told Yurt, the oldest boy, to look after him.

"Magnifico needs me," she explained. "He's going to go adventuring one day and bring back gold and jewels and a princess, and we're all going to live Happily Ever After in Glorious Luxury."

"OK, Ma." Yurt nodded. "What's the baby's name?"

Aggie Onion looked blank. "Don't ask me. I've already had to think of seven names. You think of something."

Yurt studied the baby. "Alfie," he said, and Alfie Onion it was.

Chapter Two

FOURTEEN YEARS LATER, an unusual smell of baking filled the kitchen at Pigsticking Farm.

"There!" Aggie Onion banged the plate down on the table. "Look at that!"

"Cake!" breathed Yurt. "WOW!"

"WOW!" echoed six of his seven younger brothers.

The cake was small, lumpy and burnt. All the same, it was a cake, and cakes were hardly ever seen in Pigsticking Farm. The wife of a pig farmer for eighteen years, Aggie was limited in her ingredients; sausages, pork pies, ham sandwiches and bacon butties were her usual offerings.

"And it's got icing!" Kip's eyes were very wide.

Whelk, Kip's twin, leant over the table to look. "Icing with writing on!"

Yurt spelt it out. "Good luck Magnifico!"

Mrs Onion wiped her hands on her greasy apron and smiled proudly. "Special day, today," she said. "Celebrating, that's what we're doing! Celebrating our happy hero."

Seven pairs of eyes turned to look. The hero was slumped at the head of the table. Under his substantial bottom was a well-worn velvet cushion, and a piece of tarnished tinsel was wound in and out of the chair back. The expression on his face suggested that he was far from happy.

Mrs Onion produced a knife and carefully cut the cake down the middle.

"This afternoon," she announced, "our Magnifico goes adventuring!"

She put half the cake on the hero's plate, then divided the other half into six slices.

"What about Alfie, Ma?" Yurt asked.

His mother looked annoyed. "Makes it awkward, seven slices," she said. "Alf doesn't mind, do you Alf?"

Alfie shook his head. "I don't mind, Ma."

Under the table Bowser, Alfie's dog, growled angrily. He'd seen Alfie being left out far too often, and he didn't think it was right. "**Unfair unfair unfairrrrrr**,"
he muttered. Fortunately, Alfie was the only one who understood him.

"Ssh!" he warned. "I don't mind. Not really."

Once the cake had been eaten, Aggie stomped over

to a cupboard and flung open the door, revealing a large paper parcel tied up with string. "Been saving these for years and years," she said. "And now the time's come at last. Stand up, Magnifico, and we'll get you ready."

Magnifico stared at his mother. "What? What do you mean?"

Aggie beamed fondly at her favourite son. "You've got to be dressed right for adventuring. It's like I said, today's the day. It's the seventh day of the seventh month, and YOU, Magnifico Onion, are the seventh son of a seventh son. You're going off to win the hand of a lovely princess, and you'll soon be back home with a fortune. Pots and pots of gold – and we'll all be able to live in Glorious Luxury. Every single one of us!"

"Even Alfie?" Yurt asked.

Aggie nodded. "Even Alfie."

Alfie's eyes opened wide in astonishment. "So I won't have to sleep in the barn?"

The glowing vision of the future made Aggie unusually generous. "You'll have your very own bed," she promised.

"WOW!" Alfie jumped up and flung his arms round his mother. "Thank you, Ma!"

"It's Magnifico you'll have to thank for it," Aggie told him as she pushed him away, but her tone was gentler than usual. "He's the one who's going to make us all rich."

She turned to the cupboard and heaved the paper parcel off the shelf. Dumping it on the table among the crumbs, she undid the string with a flourish. "There we are! Hat and boots with silver buckles."

Magnifico looked uneasily at the boots. "They look a bit small, Ma."

"It's what a hero wears," Aggie said firmly. "It says so in my book." She was back in the cupboard. "And look here! A real hero's sword!"

Yurt sniggered. "That's a bread knife."

Aggie was not to be put off. "It's as good as a sword any day. Your dad spent an age sharpening it."

The hero blinked. "Why do I need a sword?"

Aggie Onion folded her arms. "Now, now,

Magnifico. I've read you those stories a hundred times. You've got to find your princess, and you might meet trolls or a couple of ogres along the way."

Magnifico was pale green. "But I don't want to meet any ogres. Or trolls. You never said anything about trolls, Ma! You said all I had to do was find a princess and marry her and then I'd be rich and have all the chocolate I ever wanted!"

His mother patted his trembling arm. "Don't you worry, pet," she soothed. "You're the seventh son of a seventh son. The trolls won't touch you. They'll run away as soon as they know who you are."

"But what if they eat me before I can tell them?" Magnifico was greener than ever. "They might be hiding behind a bush, and pounce on me when I'm not looking! How will they know I'm a hero if I'm being munched and crunched and gobbled?"

Things were not going quite as Aggie Onion had hoped. She tried to think if any of her stories featured an unwilling hero, and something stirred in her memory.

"I know," she said. "Take Alfie with you, and he can go on ahead and explain who you are. Lots of heroes have a Faithful Servant. It's usually a dog. Or a horse. But I expect Alfie would do."

Magnifico brightened visibly, and Alfie stared at the ground, hopeful butterflies fluttering in his chest. He didn't dare say a word; any sign that he really, really, REALLY wanted to go on an adventure might make his mother change her mind, or make his brother refuse to take him.

Aggie was still considering her idea. The more she thought about it, the better it appeared. "Alfie can carry the luggage," she said. "And it'll get him out from under my feet. What do you think, Magnifico? Would you like a Faithful Servant?"

Magnifico, terrified of being sent off on his own but not wanting Alfie to think he was needed, did his best to look as if he was doing his brother a favour. "I suppose he can come."

"Do you promise to do everything you can to help your brother?" Aggie gave Alfie a stern look.

Alfie nodded. "Cross my heart and hope to die!"

He meant it. Success would mean his very own bed, and, for someone who slept on a pile of hay in the barn, that was Glorious Luxury indeed.

And so it was decided: Alfie was to travel with Magnifico. While the hero was being dressed in his hat, cloak and boots, Alfie collected his few belongings and tied them up in a handkerchief.

Under the table, Bowser sat up. If Alfie was going out adventuring, then he was going too. He glanced round the kitchen, saw nothing he wanted, and went to wait for Alfie outside the front door.

Garf was too busy with his pigs to say goodbye, but Aggie Onion and her boys stood in a line to wish the hero good fortune, good luck and speedy success.

Aggie was torn between tears and an ecstatic smile; her beloved seventh son was leaving home, but he was going to bring her a Happily Ever After and Glorious Luxury. The brothers shuffled their feet and slapped Magnifico on the back. Only Yurt gave Alfie a quick pat as he followed Magnifico down the line. "Here." He slid a small parcel into Alfie's pocket. "This might come in useful. Take care of yourself!"

Alfie grinned. "Thanks."

Their mother snorted. "It's our Magnifico he should be taking care of, not himself! And make sure you do, Alf. I don't want to hear that your brother's been eaten and you haven't!"

"No, Ma." Alfie gave his mother what he hoped was an I'm-happy-to-be-eaten smile, and she gave him a half-hearted wave before clasping Magnifico to her bosom for one last farewell hug.

Five minutes later they were on their way, Alfie in front staggering under the weight of several bulging picnic baskets, which were to keep the hero from starvation, and a couple of leather cases containing

the hero's clothes. Bowser walked beside him, his tail wagging as he thought of the adventures to come. Magnifico stomped in the rear, glancing nervously to the left and right as he went, as if he was already expecting to see trolls and ogres.

Chapter Three

WALKING ALONG THE LANE that led away from
Pigsticking Farm, Alfie was happier than he'd ever
been. He was going on an adventure! And Bowser
was coming with him. And there would be (as far
as he could tell) no washing up or clothes to scrub,
although he supposed that Magnifico might demand
clean socks from time to time. He began to whistle,
but was immediately hushed by his brother.

"What if the trolls hear us?"

Alfie laughed. "Why would there be trolls here?
Pa walks along this road every time he takes the pigs
to market, and he's never met a troll."

"They could be hiding in the ditch," Magnifico said. "Hiding and waiting for a hero to walk past."

Alfie snapped his fingers. "Bowser! Go search!"

Bowser bounded off to the side of the road, and sniffed in the ditch. "**All clear!**" he barked. "**All clear all clear all clear!**"

"There," Alfie said. "Bowser says it's all clear, so you've nothing to worry about."

Magnifico frowned. "I do wish you wouldn't pretend you understand that stupid animal every time he barks. He's a dog. Dogs don't talk."

Alfie knew it was useless to explain that he understood everything Bowser said. He shrugged, and went to look himself. "Nothing there. No trolls."

Magnifico wasn't convinced. "That doesn't mean there aren't any. Even if Pa does come this way, he isn't a hero, is he? So they wouldn't want to eat him. And I hope they don't eat you, either. What if the princess is up at the top of a crumbling tower? I hate heights, so I'll need you to fetch her down. And I'm certainly not going to carry my own luggage!"

"Oh." Alfie would have rubbed his nose if his arms hadn't been full of cases and baskets. "But … but isn't it the hero who does the rescuing? I don't think I want to marry a princess."

Magnifico gave him a scornful look. "You know what? You're really, REALLY stupid! Of course the hero gets the princess, and I'M the hero. But you're my Faithful Servant, so you do the rescuing. Now, let's have a rest. My feet hurt."

"OK." Alfie put the cases and baskets down under a tree. "I'll go and have a look along the road. If there's a cart coming, we could hitch a ride. I won't be long. Bowser'll keep you company."

He saw Magnifico beginning to frown, and added, "You could have a pie, or something."

The frown changed to a smile, and Magnifico sat down happily beside the largest basket.

"I suppose I could. A hero has to keep his strength up." A moment later he was tucking into a large pork pie.

Up in the tree above the hero's head, two magpies were watching and listening.

"Well, well, well!" The sleeker of the two birds winked a sharp black eye. "Perce, old buddy – what do you reckon to that?"

Perce sighed. "It's only a pork pie, Kev."

"Pie? There's a HERO wrapped round it, feather brain. And do you know what heroes do?"

Perce paused. He was sure this was a trick question, but he couldn't see how. "They eat pies?" he offered.

Kev groaned. "No! They go on adventures."

"Ah." Perce looked doubtful. "That's good, is it?"

His companion rolled his eyes. "Good? GOOD? It's the biggest stroke of luck we've ever had! He'll be looking for gold, and lots and lots of shiny sparkly treasure." Kev closed his eyes in rapture at the thought. "Perce, we're made! At last!"

"If you say so." Perce fluffed his feathers and began to shuffle away.

"Oi! Where are you going?" Kev asked. "You're on duty, as from now!"

"No, Kev," Perce protested.

Kev gave him a chilling look. "Too bad, old chum! You're needed. Humans see one of us and it's, 'Oh! Oh! Oh! One for sorrow!' But two of us? They LOVE it!" He put his head on one side, and recited,

> *"One for sorrow, two for joy,*
> *Three for a girl and four for a boy,*
> *Five for silver, six for gold,*
> *Seven for a secret never to be told.*

"And they believe it, Perce! Every word. So you stay with me, you hear?"

Perce shrugged. "Don't want to."

"Come on, buddy," Kev said. "I've got twitchy tail feathers – that's the best sign ever!"

Perce shrugged again. "Don't care."

Kev changed tack. "Perce, dear old friend … you don't want to spend the rest of your life thinking you lost your poor mate Kev a fortune, do you?"

Perce sighed heavily, and shrugged one last time. "Oh … all right. But no funny business, mind!"

"Me? Funny business?" Kev was deeply shocked. "Never. Now, keep your peepers open! We're going to hang around this guy…"

Chapter Four

ALFIE WAS BACK REMARKABLY QUICKLY. He had seen a hay cart trundling along the road, and had persuaded the farmer to give them a lift.

Magnifico looked up with a scowl. "You're back much too soon, stupid. I haven't nearly finished my picnic."

"But don't you want a ride, Maggers?" Alfie asked.

"I suppose," his brother said ungraciously. He stuffed a pie into his mouth and washed it down with lemonade. "There," he said. "That'll have to do, I suppose. I'm still hungry, but we can stop again soon. I'll tell you when. Oh, and I've been thinking.

If you're my Faithful Servant, you shouldn't call me Maggers." He puffed out his chest. "I think you should call me Master. Or Sir."

Bowser sat bolt upright.

"**What what WHAT?**"

Alfie shook his head at the dog. "Hush, Bowser. I don't mind."

"I don't mind, MASTER!" Magnifico corrected.

Alfie grinned. "I don't mind, Master."

"**Not right!**" Bowser was furious. "**Not right NOT RIGHT!**"

"It's only a word," Alfie told him. "It doesn't mean anything." He bent down and picked up the luggage. "Off we go adventuring, Master."

Magnifico looked at him suspiciously. "Are you laughing at me?"

Alfie shook his head. "Of course not, Master."

He swung the baskets and cases onto his back and set off towards the hay cart, the indignant Bowser at his heels. Magnifico, with an effort, got to his feet. His boots, although undoubtedly heroic in appearance, were too tight, and he winced as he waddled after his brother.

"Oi!" he shouted. "Don't go so fast!"

It took all of Alfie's strength to push Magnifico onto the cart, but at last he was safely settled. As Alfie sat down beside his brother, something hard in his back pocket made him uncomfortable; pulling it out, he found Yurt's parcel and he opened it with interest. Inside was his brother's best catapult. Knowing how much time Yurt had spent making it, Alfie smiled happily as he tucked it away.

"What's that?" Magnifico asked.

"Just a catapult," Alfie told him. "Might come in useful..."

The farmer cracked his whip and away they went, rolling past small cottages and green fields. Gradually the scenery changed: the trees were taller, the houses fewer, the fields wider ... and then came wilder countryside, with craggy rocks, boggy marshes and one small, lonely farmhouse.

"Here's as far as I go," the farmer said gruffly. "Down you get!"

The hero and his Faithful Servant climbed down. Alfie thanked the farmer, Magnifico grunted, and the two of them set off along the road that was now much narrower and rougher.

"Look, Maggers!" Alfie said. "There's a bridge ahead. That must be the River Dribble. They say weird and wonderful things happen beyond there."

This was not what the hero wanted to hear. He crossed the bridge one step at a time, looking over his shoulder and shivering. Once he reached the other side he sat down on a tussock under a willow tree and stretched out his portly legs.

"My boots are uncomfortable," he complained. "I'm getting blisters." He eyed Alfie's well-worn hand-me-downs. "Maybe we should swap."

"If you like." Alfie pulled off a battered boot, but when a large hole was revealed in the sole his brother had a change of heart.

He waved his hand in a grandiloquent gesture. "You can keep them."

Alfie bowed low. "Thank you, kind Master."

Magnifico's face darkened. "You're laughing at me again, and I won't have it! When I'm rich and married to a princess I'm not going to give you a penny. So there! And I hope you DO get eaten by an ogre – after you've rescued the princess, of course."

Alfie could hear Bowser beginning to mutter about **mean mean mean** brothers, and he put out a hand to soothe the angry dog. "It's OK, Bowser. Shall we get going again, Master?"

His brother nodded in a distracted way; a sound above his head had made him look up. "Huh," he said. "Horrible birds. Can't even sing."

Alfie gave the magpies a silent cheer. "Two magpies! That's good luck. 'One for sorrow, two for joy.' They've come to tell you you're going to find a princess, Master! You're going to be a huge success!"

"H'mph," was all Magnifico said, but he got to his feet and started walking.

*   *   *

Progress was slow, as Magnifico's boots grew more and more painful. The afternoon sun was low in the sky before they came to a wide marshy plain dotted with clumps of reeds, twisted trees and thorny bushes. In the distance a dark forest loomed. Alfie greeted the sight with enthusiasm. "A deep dark forest … at last! That's where adventures always happen!"

Magnifico shuddered. "Where's the castle?" he asked plaintively. "We don't have to spend the night away from home, do we?"

Alfie looked at him in surprise. "Didn't you listen

when Ma was reading you all those stories? Sometimes the hero seeks his fortune for years and years."

The hero glared at him. "Don't tell fibs! Ma said I'd be back in no time at all!"

"She wouldn't have packed so many picnics if she thought you were coming home this evening," Alfie pointed out. "Or two cases of clothes."

The truth of this hit Magnifico with a hideous jolt. He sank down on the road and looked pleadingly at Alfie. "But I don't want to be away for years! I don't want to be away for a month! Or even a week! My feet hurt and I'm scared of trolls and ogres and … and all that kind of thing. Can't you go and fetch the princess for me? Erm … please?"

Alfie sighed. He couldn't help feeling sorry for Magnifico, who was red in the face and sweating.

"I would if I could," he said. "But it has to be you. It's the seventh son of a seventh son who has the magic powers, not the eighth."

Magnifico drooped even more and put his head in his hands. "I wish I was dead."

Alfie rubbed his nose while he tried to think of a way of encouraging his brother to keep going. Bowser came to stand beside him. "**Shame shame shame**," he remarked. "**Long road road road ahead.**" He stared into the distance – and his tail suddenly started wagging furiously. "**Look look LOOK!**"

Alfie's eyesight was nothing like as good as Bowser's, and it was another couple of minutes before he was able to make out the figures moving towards them. He stared, shut his eyes, opened them and looked again.

It was a man driving a horse and cart. The cart was bright green, and painted on the sides was a sign:

J. JONES
ANYTHING BOUGHT, ANYTHING SOLD.
I TRAVEL NORTH, SOUTH, EAST AND WEST.

Behind the cart, on the end of a rope, trailed another horse – a curious looking animal patched in black and white. Round its neck hung a board:

FOR SALE
ANY OFFERS CONSIDERED. NO REFUNDS.

An idea popped into Alfie's head. Would J. Jones swap the piebald horse? There was an enormous bag of pork pies in one of the baskets, but would they be enough? It was worth trying.

"Maggers – I mean, Master – I've got a brilliant idea! Wait here, I'll be back in no time. Take off your boots, and eat something. Bowser, on guard!"

Before his brother could object, Alfie had grabbed the bag and was running up the road. Magnifico, outraged, shook his fist, but investigation of the second picnic basket made him think that Alfie was right. It was important to keep his strength up; a couple of thick-cut ham and pickle sandwiches and a substantial sausage would make a reasonable snack. Bowser settled himself on top of the luggage and waited to see what would happen next.

*   *   *

Kev, uncomfortably perched in a gorse bush beside
a dozing Perce, shifted from foot to foot. He'd been
watching Magnifico for long enough to discover that the
hero was an interesting character. Greed, self-interest,
lack of consideration for others – all qualities Kev was
inclined to admire. He was, however, puzzled by Alfie.
What was in it for the boy? And, more importantly,
what could Kev and Perce get out of the fact that a
cowardly hero was on his way to find a princess?

"There's a deal to be made," Kev muttered.
"Brilliant brain like mine … sure to find an answer
soon. Keep listening—"

"AWK?" Perce opened a bleary eye. "What's up?"

"Not much." Kev tweaked at a tail feather. "The
hero's eating again. The brother's gone racing up the
road to chat to a guy with a cart and a couple of nags.
Get your beauty sleep while you can, buddy. Gotta
feeling it's all about to kick off."

Chapter Five

ALFIE, AS HE CAME CLOSER, noticed that the piebald horse was behaving in a curious way. It kept peering from side to side, and occasionally it let out a loud whinny. It would then do a little dance, and follow this by nodding its head up and down as if acknowledging applause. When it saw Alfie it stopped, and the two of them inspected each other with interest.

J. Jones leant down from his cart. "Want to buy a horse, laddie? Dirt cheap, but absolutely, definitely NO return if found unsatisfactory."

The piebald horse gave Alfie a cheerful wink and held up a hoof in greeting.

"There you go," J. Jones said. "Adeline's taken a fancy to you. Can't say no to her now, can you?"

Alfie studied Adeline. She was old and plump, but she was in much better condition than the ancient animal pulling the cart. "Erm … if you don't mind my asking, why are you selling her?"

"One's all I need," J. Jones said, a little too quickly. "Don't want to be greedy! My dear old Boris is quite enough for me. You'd look good on a horse, you would."

Adeline nodded agreement, waggled her ears at Alfie and then, with a sudden jerk of her head, pulled the rope free of the cart. Making her way to Alfie's side, she laid a heavy head on his shoulder and breathed in a carroty whisper, "Buy me, there's a dear good boy!"

Alfie jumped. He understood Bowser's every word but, as far as he was aware, nobody else did – and he'd never expected to meet another animal who could talk.

"I'm afraid I don't have much money," he said. This was an exaggeration: he had no money at all. "But I do have a bag of the very best pork pies. Made by my mother, and she's an expert!"

"I'll trade you." J. Jones peered into the bag. "H'm. Excellent looking pies! And I'm hungry. Extremely

hungry. Give us your hand, young man. The horse is yours."

"Shake his hand, dear boy," Adeline advised. "I'm everyone's dream travelling companion – educated, cheerful, chatty.

Everyone except J. Jones, of course."

Alfie hesitated. How would Magnifico feel about a talking horse? And what would Adeline think of Magnifico?

"Oh, for goodness' sake!" Adeline tossed her head. "I'm yours, the pies are his. Look – he's eating one already!" With an emphatic nod she pushed past Alfie, made her way towards the other horse, and twitched her ears. "So long, Boris, you dear old thing." She gave Boris a friendly nip on the neck, then turned back to Alfie. "Come along, then."

"Just a minute." Alfie took a deep breath and, still unable to believe what seemed to be an extraordinary stroke of fortune, looked at J. Jones. "So … is it really OK? I take Adeline?"

J. Jones shook his hand. "It's a deal, but I'll give you a word of warning. Nothing but trouble, that one. Good luck, young feller, is what I say to you. You'll need it."

He shook the reins, and the cart went rattling down the road.

Adeline snorted. "A very small-minded man, dear boy. Another twenty-four hours of his company and I'd have gone utterly and completely mad. He hadn't the slightest interest in my opinions." She peered at Alfie. "I don't suppose you've met many horses like me, have you?"

"None," Alfie told her. "Where I come from, animals don't talk. Although I do understand Bowser, and he understands me."

"Bowser? Who's he?"

"He's my dog," Alfie said.

"Oh, a dog!" Adeline evidently approved of dogs. "Intelligent animals, dogs."

Alfie was about to agree, but was distracted by the sudden sound of raised voices. Swinging round, he saw Magnifico waving his arms and shouting at J. Jones, who was eating his second pork pie.

"Oops," Alfie said. "I bet Maggers thinks Mr Jones has stolen his pies. I'd better go and explain."

Adeline raised an eyebrow. "Maggers?"

"My brother. He's a hero."

Alfie began running down the road, and Adeline trotted after him.

"Doesn't look much like a hero to me," she said. "I understood they were tall, dark and handsome. That one's small, pink and decidedly—"

"I'll introduce you!" Alfie hastily interrupted the horse before she could say anything too rude. "Magnifico's the seventh son of a seventh son. And he's going to marry a princess ... well, he is when we find one."

Magnifico, hearing his name, turned round to glare at Alfie. "Why are you never here when you're needed? This man's stolen a bag of my favourite pork pies!"

"It's OK," Alfie soothed. "I swapped the pies for this ... this magnificent animal! Her name's Adeline. So now you'll be able to ride, and your boots won't hurt you any more."

Magnifico switched his gaze to Adeline, and Adeline stared back.

"H'm," the hero said. "She's very skinny."

Adeline looked down her nose. "And you're very—"

"SPLENDID!" Alfie cut in. "He's very splendid, aren't you, Master?"

Alfie needn't have bothered to try to save his brother's feelings. Magnifico was goggle-eyed.

"Did … did it SPEAK?"

"Of course I did," Adeline snapped. "And we'd better come to an understanding, you and I. You may or may not be a hero – after all, I've only got this boy's word for it – but one thing I will not tolerate is personal remarks. Is that understood?"

Magnifico hadn't heard a word. He was still staring.

Alfie stood on tiptoe to whisper in Adeline's ear. "He's a bit – erm – in awe of you at the moment."

"Is that so?" The piebald horse's anger evaporated. "I am a rather remarkable animal. Do I gather you're expecting this hero of yours to ride on my back, by the way? I don't remember that being mentioned when we met."

Alfie looked apologetic. "I … I sort of thought you'd take it for granted."

"Learn an important lesson, dear boy," Adeline said. "Never take anything for granted." She peered at Magnifico. "How much does he weigh?"

Magnifico blinked in surprise. "Pardon?"

"I have a weight limit," Adeline explained. "And you're a substantial kind of chap." She walked round the hero who, for the second time in two minutes, was speechless. "H'm. Excuse me while I consult Norman and Penelope. They're hitching a ride with me. A sensible pair." She gave a high-pitched whistle, and two white mice popped their heads out of a small bag tied to her saddle. "Norman, ducky – what do you think? Can we accommodate this young man? What do you say, Penelope?"

"Too big," Norman squeaked, and disappeared again.

Penelope was slower to make up her mind. "He's nearly at the limit," she remarked, "but I'd say you can do it, darling."

Adeline nodded. "That's what I thought."

Penelope twitched her whiskers. "Pardon my mentioning it, but did you know there's a DOG asleep on top of those bags over there?"

"A dog? Oh yes. Property of the boy, I believe." Adeline turned to look. "Alfie, do tell … what are your companion's feelings on the subject of mice?"

Perce was leaning so far forward he was in danger of falling off his twig. "Look at that, Kev! It's a right old party down there. Can't we join in?"

Kev looked at his companion in alarm. "Oi! Stop it! We're in this for the dosh, cash, silver, gold and the twinkly sparkly shiny stuff – and we don't know yet which side we're on! Don't you go getting any of your softie ideas now. That red-faced one down there is the seventh son of a seventh son, and whatever you might think of him he's got something special ... he's what we in the trade call a saleable commodity."

Perce blinked. "Awk?"

"Something worth selling," Kev translated. "Now, button up and listen!"

Chapter Six

ALFIE RUBBED HIS NOSE, which always helped him think, and grinned. This was a very different world, and he was beginning to enjoy it. Talking horses, talking mice ... and nobody telling him to go and scrub floors or peel potatoes. He looked hopefully at Bowser. Would the dog speak?

Bowser got to his feet and shook himself. Then he sat down again and scratched his ear.

"**Mice?**" he said. "**Mice mice mice? Not a problem. No no no. Don't eat mice. Rats? GRRRRRRR!!! Oh yes yes YES. And cheese. Cheese is good good good!**" He gave Alfie a fond look. "**He shares bread and cheese cheese cheese with me.**"

Penelope nodded. "Glad to hear it. May I introduce myself? Penelope Longtail, temporarily homeless and temporarily residing in our horsey friend's saddlebag. The other mouse—" she pointed to the spot where Norman had vanished— "is my brother Norman. Grumpy and generally unpleasant, but clever. Very clever."

Much to Alfie's delight, Bowser made a low bow. "**Pleasure to meet you. Bowser dog dog dog, at your service. Friend of Alfie Onion.**" He gave Adeline a thoughtful glance. "**Best best BEST friend of Alfie Onion.**"

Penelope curtsied. "Lovely, darling. I can tell we're going to get on famously." She leant forward and tweaked Adeline's mane. "Where are your manners, Addy?"

Adeline threw up her head. "Ouch! That hurt!" She looked across at Bowser. "Adeline. That's me."

"Just a minute!" Magnifico was standing in his

too tight boots and pinching himself as he stared first at Adeline, then Bowser, and then Penelope. "Is this some kind of horrible trick or something?"

Alfie threw out his arms. "This is adventuring, Master!"

"Well, I don't like it." Magnifico was frowning heavily. "Tell them to be quiet."

"I don't think I will, actually," Alfie said, rather astonished at his own bravery in standing up to his brother. "I think they're nice."

Adeline gave Magnifico a cold look. "Alfie, dear boy, are you sure you want to go travelling with this offensive young person?"

"He's not used to adventures," Alfie explained. "And I have to go with him. Ma would be furious if I didn't! She's been waiting for years and years and years for him to bring home a princess and a royal fortune so she and Pa can give up the pig farm and live Happily Ever After in Glorious Luxury."

Magnifico's face had been growing redder and redder as he listened. Now he stamped his foot and glowered at Alfie. "Don't talk such rubbish! It'll be MY Glorious Luxury, not Ma's. And I can do what I want with it!" He turned to face Adeline. "I don't care if you're a talking horse or a singing rabbit. I'm the seventh son of a seventh son, and I'm SPECIAL! I'm going to find a princess and be rich and famous … and if Alfie won't help me, then I'm going on my own. And if I get eaten by a troll it'll be all his fault! So there!"

He picked up the largest picnic basket and limped off along the road.

"Whoops," Alfie said, and he started to gather up the rest of the luggage.

"Dear boy – what are you doing?" Adeline asked.

"Going after him." Alfie swung the cases onto his back. "I promised Ma."

Adeline sighed. "I had a nasty suspicion you were a boy who kept his promises. Oh well. Let's go."

It only took a few minutes to reach Magnifico. He looked round as Alfie arrived, and scowled. "So you decided to do as you were told!"

"Shall I help you get on Adeline?" Alfie asked. "We'll travel much faster."

The hero folded his arms. "What about those mice? I don't like mice!"

"And WE don't like YOU!" It was Norman, who had popped his head out of the saddlebag.

"Do be quiet, Norm," Penelope told him. She ran lightly along Adeline's back and pirouetted on the pommel of the saddle. "You won't see us, darling," she promised Magnifico. "You won't even know we're here!"

"Yes I will," he retorted. He turned to Alfie. "Get rid of them! Feed them to your stupid dog! And tell them to stop calling me darling!"

Alfie put the luggage down and went to stand in front of his brother. "Look here, Maggers," he said. "Do you want to find a princess or not?"

The hero pouted. "Don't be silly. Of course I do!"

"Good." Alfie opened the picnic basket lying beside Magnifico and handed him a bag of sticky currant buns. "You have something to eat, and I'll talk to Norman and Penelope."

Magnifico snatched the bag. "Hurry up, then."

Adeline was watching the brothers, her lip curled in disgust. "Alfie, dear boy! Just leave the little toad here, and you and I will go out into the world with your dog. Think what fun we could have!"

Alfie sighed. It was a tempting offer, but he couldn't accept. Even though Aggie Onion had ignored him for most of his life, he felt sorry for her.

She had pinned her hopes on Magnifico for so long that her world would collapse if the hero didn't find his princess. She needed her Happily Ever After...

"Thanks," he said, "but I have to look after him."

"We'll help you, darling." It was Penelope, looking at him with her bright little eyes. "And you're quite right to stand by him. I've got an idea ... why don't we travel with you instead of in Adeline's saddlebag? A boy's shoulder gives a mouse a fine view of the world!" She glanced down at Bowser. "Would you mind, my friend?"

Bowser shook his furry head. "**Not not not at all. Pleasure pleasure pleasure!**"

There was an angry squeak from the saddlebag. "A boy's shoulder? I'll catch my death of cold! What's wrong with a nice warm pocket?"

"You can ride in my pocket if you like," Alfie said. "I don't mind."

Adeline gave him a disapproving stare and blew down her nose. "I suppose you're expecting me to carry that self-centred brother of yours?"

"Yes please," Alfie said. "I think we ought to try to get to the forest before dark."

The piebald horse nodded. "Nothing like a deep dark forest in the dark dark night for finding an adventure." She lowered her voice. "Have you noticed, dear boy? We've got company!"

"Company?" Alfie, startled, looked round. "What kind of company?"

"Magpies. There's a couple of them in that willow tree over there, and they've been following us."

"There were two magpies on the road to the village as well," Alfie said. "They're not dangerous, are they?"

Adeline looked horrified. "Dear boy, you're adventuring! ANYTHING can be dangerous. Spies come in all shapes and sizes, you know."

Alfie turned to glance at the willow tree, but he could see nothing.

"Maybe they're looking out for us," he said. "Maybe they want to be friends."

"Maybe yes, and maybe no." Adeline gave the tree a thoughtful look. "Time will tell, dear boy."

In the willow tree, there was consternation.

"Kev! We've been rumbled!" Perce's feathers were sticking up on end in agitation. "She said SPIES, Kev!"

"Stay cool, buddy." Kev was much less ruffled. "We aren't spies yet, because we don't know who we're spying for. So that makes us just – what's the word? Observers."

Perce looked hopeful. "Is that something to do with eggs? I once found a nice fresh hen's egg … it was so lovely…"

"Watchers, feather-brain. That's what we are – watchers." Kev nodded. "Although I might just be thinking of a clever idea. A VERY clever idea!"

Chapter Seven

As Alfie helped Norman into his pocket, and Penelope onto his shoulder, Magnifico looked up from his third bun. "Oi! Are we going to go adventuring or not?"

Adeline walked over to him. "Did nobody ever tell you, young man, that 'please' is a remarkably helpful word? As, indeed, is 'thank you'."

"Whatever." Magnifico picked up a fourth bun, considered it, then put it back in the bag. "So where's the ladder?"

"Ladder?" Alfie stared at his brother.

The hero pointed at Adeline's saddle. "How else am I going to get up into that seat thing? And it doesn't look very comfortable. Can't you find a cushion?"

It took some time to get Magnifico seated on Adeline's back. Not having a ladder, Alfie had to persuade the hero to scramble to the top of a low wall and then crawl across. Magnifico was certain he was about to fall to his death, and he squealed and protested until he was finally in place.

Then, as Adeline started walking, he began to wail again. "It's dangerous! I don't like it. Stop! Stop!"

Adeline ignored him. She kept moving at a steady pace, and Alfie half-walked, half-ran beside her. Penelope, on Alfie's shoulder, winked at Bowser, who was running behind. "Such fun, darling – so much more entertaining than J. Jones."

Adeline heard her. "What a fool that man was. And so unobservant. Why, we walked right past the most enormous troll – and he never even noticed!"

"TROLL?" Alfie stopped dead. Magnifico began to tremble.

"Oh yes, dear boy. The forest's full of them."

Adeline sounded so casual that Alfie took a moment to take in the full importance of what she had said. When he did, a huge smile spread over his face. "Wow!" he said. "WOW!"

The hero was the colour of old cheese. "So we oughtn't go there at night. Not at all. No way."

Penelope leant forward. "But what about the princess, darling? The princess in the enchanted castle in the middle of the trees?"

There was a sudden silence.

"Princess?" Magnifico's voice was now a squeak. "There's a PRINCESS in the forest?"

"A very pretty one," Penelope said.

"Is she rich?" the hero asked eagerly. "Loads of cash? Pots and pots and pots of gold?"

The mouse gave him a thoughtful stare. "Does it matter?"

Magnifico was appalled. "Does it matter? Of COURSE it matters! If she hasn't got money I'm not interested. Not at all." He puffed out his chest. "Only the best will do for Magnifico Onion!"

"Fancy that," Penelope said. "What a lucky princess she'll be."

Magnifico looked at Alfie. "Is she laughing at me? I don't want to be laughed at!"

Alfie ignored him and turned to Bowser and Adeline. "I think we'll go as far as the edge of the forest, and make a camp for the night." He paused. "And then I might just go and have a little wander round…"

"No no NO!" Magnifico's face was green with

terror. "You'll get gobbled up by a troll and then I won't have anyone to look after me. You can't, I won't allow it!"

Nothing Alfie said would calm his brother, and in the end he was forced to promise that he would make no attempt to explore the forest until the following day. Only then would Magnifico go on.

"It could be for the best, darling," Penelope whispered in Alfie's ear as Adeline walked away, the hero clinging to her neck. "Most of the trolls are absolutely harmless – some are quite pleasant, in fact – but one or two get a little overexcited when the moon is up."

"And is there really a princess in an enchanted castle?" Alfie asked. "And does she really need rescuing?"

The little white mouse nodded. "She's asleep, darling. She's been asleep for ages and ages and ages, and the castle's completely surrounded by thorns."

"Oh, I know that story!" Alfie's eyes shone. "It was one of my mother's favourites. Someone has to hack down the thorns and kiss her, and then she'll wake up." His eyes grew brighter still. "That's such good news! I can hack down the thorns, and then Maggers can go marching in and kiss her. Even he can kiss a sleeping princess!"

"That might well be true," Penelope agreed. "But there's one small problem – apart from the thorns, of course."

Alfie stared at her. "What is it?"

"It's a blooming great ogre and his blooming great lump of a son!" Norman's head had popped out of Alfie's pocket, his whiskers quivering angrily. "They've set up camp right in front of the castle, and every time a prince comes riding up – all pleased with himself and thinking he's on his way to win a princess – out they come and bop him on the head. What do you say to that, sunshine?"

Chapter Eight

As Alfie walked along the road behind Adeline,
Bowser at his side, he was wondering just how much
he should tell his brother. He couldn't even begin to
imagine what Magnifico would say if he thought there
was one ogre, let alone two…

"Three," Penelope said.

"Three?" Alfie looked at her in surprise, and
Bowser pricked up his ears.

"You were thinking about the ogres, darling."
Penelope nodded her little head. "I could tell. And I
thought you should know that there are three of them.
There's a daughter as well. They've left her at home in

a horrible smelly old house on the edge of the forest – but she often comes to see her brother and father. She's always wandering around singing loud ogreish songs. It drives the trolls mad, because they like to sleep during the day."

"So why don't they chase her away?" Alfie asked.

Penelope shrugged. "They're scared. Ogres are strong. Strong, and stupid, and hungry. They've been known to catch little trolls and make them into pies."

Alfie shuddered. "Why didn't they catch Mr Jones, then?"

"Oh, he and Adeline travelled along the outer road," Penelope explained. "The castle's right in the middle."

Alfie rubbed his nose thoughtfully. "Can I ask you something?"

The mouse waved a paw. "Anything, darling!"

"How come you know so much about the forest?" Alfie hoped he wasn't being rude, or too inquisitive.

"We used to live there," Penelope told him, and her ears and whiskers drooped. "We had a dear little house under the thorns of Rosewall Castle, but one dreadful day we came home, darling, and it was all squashed flat! An ogre must have trodden on it. The trolls would never do anything like that. We couldn't find another house that we knew would be safe – so we decided to see the world a little, and go back when the ogres had gone. We hitched a ride with Adeline, and here we are!"

"And we wish we weren't," Norman put in. He came a little further out of Alfie's pocket, his nose twitching. "I liked living in the forest. Someone needs to get rid of those ogres! Naming no names, of course." He gave Alfie a heavy wink. "I hate them, the trolls hate them … they're no use to anyone."

Alfie was sure that Norman was right. He also had a suspicion that the mouse thought that he, Alfie Onion, was the person to remove the ogres, even though he was nobody special. Dealing with ogres was the job of a hero – but it surely needed a very different hero to the one currently riding towards the forest in his undersized boots.

Alfie sighed and looked round for Bowser. When things were getting complicated, the dog was always a comfort.

"**Run run run?**" Bowser had no problem with a little cowardice when it seemed like the safest course of action. In his opinion, ogres were best avoided.

"I suppose we could go a bit faster," Alfie agreed, and he quickened his pace.

The dog looked surprised – that wasn't what he'd had in mind – but there was a mouse-sized round of applause from Alfie's pocket. "That's the best idea I've heard today. It would be nice to think we'll get there before next week. I'm fed up with that so-called hero. Nothing but fuss fuss fuss, moan moan moan."

"Patience, Norman ducky!" Penelope shook her head at her brother. "We may be travelling slowly, but we'll get there in the end."

Adeline, catching the end of the mouse's sentence as Alfie came up beside her, twitched an ear. "What's that? Too slow? Want me to change up a gear or two?"

She gave a little skip and began to trot. Magnifico

gave a loud shriek of horror as he found himself
bouncing up and down, and Alfie hastily caught at
Adeline's reins.

"Maybe we could just try walking a little faster," he
suggested. "I don't think Maggers can quite cope with
trotting."

Adeline was happy to agree. "Couldn't have kept
that up for long anyway, dear boy," she said. "It's
exactly like having a sack of potatoes wobbling on
my back."

Alfie looked up at his brother. Magnifico was lying
across the saddle, his eyes screwed shut and his hands
clutching at Adeline's mane. He was whimpering
softly. "All right, Master?" Alfie asked.

"Do I look all right?" Magnifico wailed. "I want to
stop … and I want to go to bed with a hot water bottle
and a packet of biscuits!"

"We'll stop soon," Alfie promised.

"We'll tuck him up in a nice dry bed of heather,"
Adeline said. "There's a neat little hollow not far from
the edge of the forest – very cosy." She twitched her

ears and glanced up at the sky, where the blue was fading away into darkness and the first star was twinkling. "H'm … I'd say we were in for a warm summer's night. Lucky for us, eh?"

"That's it! THAT'S IT! My greatest idea ever ever ever!" Kev flew up in the air, looped a triumphant loop, and zoomed back to knock the sleeping Perce off his branch. "Wakey wakey! Rise and shine!"

"I'd rather have a nice fresh hen's egg," Perce grumbled. "What are you fussing about now?"

"Fuss? You're talking to a genius, Percy my lad. Just listen to my idea! There are ogres in those woods, right?"

Perce yawned. "If you say so."

"I do. The mouse just said. Now, that lily-livered hero's never going to make it to the princess and the gold and treasure – repeat, TREASURE, as in twinkly sparkly shiny stuff – until the ogres have gone. Right?"

Perce nodded. "Right."

"So he needs help. He needs an army. Who's got an army? The trolls. And they hate the ogres, so it's looking good. Very good! Now, you're just about to ask me why the trolls don't chase the ogres away—"

"Am I?" Perce scratched his neck. "Why?"

Kev gave an exasperated squawk. "Because that's what any bird with any sense would ask! The trolls are scared. Those ogres are big and strong. But trolls are strong too, and there are a lot more trolls than there are ogres. So what do they need? A leader! In fact, they need a hero! Get my drift?"

"Erm…" Perce said.

"Never mind. We tell the trolls there's a hero on his way to the forest. We tell them he's a right clever chap, and if they help him he'll get rid of the ogres for good and all. They help, the ogres go, the hero gets the princess and the gold – and guess what we get, Perce?"

Perce looked hopeful. "Two eggs?"

"Nah. We get twinkly sparkly shiny treasure. Enough for the rest of our little lives, Perce."

Perce shuffled on his branch. He could see a problem. "But ... but Kev! That hero – he's not clever. Not at all."

"Well spotted, my little old buddy bird. But his brother is, and so's that horse, and the mice are as bright as ninepence! They'll think of something. Not too sure about the dog, mind. But don't you worry, I've got it sorted. Off we go, ups-a-daisy!" And Kev was airborne, circling up and up into the evening sky.

Perce shook his head, and followed.

Chapter Nine

THE LITTLE PARTY TRAVELLED STEADILY ON. More stars
came out, followed by a moon that turned Adeline
into a horse of black and silver. The hero mumbled
and muttered, and when at last Adeline announced
that they had reached their destination – a small
heather-filled hollow in a circle of gorse bushes – he
announced that he wanted a proper bed.

"Maggers, there ISN'T a bed." Alfie was doing his
best to be patient. "Look … we'll light a fire so you
can keep warm while you eat your supper. And maybe
tomorrow we'll find the castle, and you can kiss the
princess, and it'll be a Happily Ever After ending!"

Magnifico had climbed down from Adeline's back, and was rubbing his bottom.

"I'm never going to be able to sit down again," he complained. "I told you I needed a cushion, but you never got me one. You're stupid and you're useless, Alfie Onion. I wish I'd never let you come with me!"

Alfie didn't answer. He handed the hero one of the picnic baskets, and began to look for sticks for a fire. Magnifico immediately forgot his aches and pains and opened a greasy paper bag with coos of pleasure. A moment later his mouth was so full of sausage roll he couldn't complain any more.

"And where's your picnic, dear boy?" Adeline enquired.

"I've got a cheese sandwich," Alfie said. "It's not all that old … Pa brought it back from work."

Adeline's snort of disgust made even Magnifico look up.

Bowser gave a short sharp yap, and bounced towards the food baskets.

"Bowser! NO!" Alfie yelled, and Magnifico let out a shriek of horror.

"Don't you DARE touch my picnics!"

Bowser took no notice. Snatching up one of the baskets he tipped it over, and three large ham pies fell out onto the grass. Magnifico crammed his sausage roll into his mouth and rushed to save his precious food – but Bowser was too quick for him. Seizing the largest pie he bounded back to Alfie, and laid it at his feet.

"**Pie pie pie!**" he said.

"Oh, Bowser…" Alfie shook a warning finger at the dog. "That belongs to Maggers. I can't eat it."

"No you jolly well can't!" Magnifico was purple with rage. "That's MY pie!" He snatched it back, glanced at it, then hurled it into the thickest gorse bush. "Yuck! It's got doggy tooth marks on it!"

"I'd have eaten it," Alfie said wistfully. "I don't mind Bowser's tooth marks."

"But it's MINE!" The hero put his hands on his hips and puffed out his chest. "It's ME who's the seventh son of the seventh son! Ma cooked those pies for me, not you!" He marched to the edge of the hollow, gathered the remaining picnic baskets together, piled them up, and sat on them.

Adeline shook her head. "Temper temper! Be careful you don't give yourself hiccups."

Alfie tried his best not to laugh, but his face gave him away. Magnifico thumped the top of a box of sandwiches. "Stop laughing! I don't like it. You know I don't, Alfie!" There was now a plaintive note in his voice, and he pouted as he helped himself to another ham pie.

"If you don't wish to be laughed at, young man," Adeline said, "don't behave like a potato pudding. If you have even a scrap of generosity, you'll give your brother something to eat." She turned her back and began to crop the grass.

"**Well said said said!**" Bowser waved a paw.

Magnifico studied the half-eaten pie in his hand. "You can have some, Alfie." He broke off a piece of crust and held it out. "Here." And he gave Adeline a triumphant glare.

"I'm overwhelmed," Adeline told him. "You've taken my breath away."

"Actually," Alfie said, "I think I'll eat my cheese sandwich, but thank you very much. Bowser, you and Penelope can share the crust. Oh, and Norman too." He sat down, and broke the pie crust into three pieces. "Here you—"

"Aaaaaaaaaaaaaaaaaaagh!" Magnifico's scream was piercing. He was pointing at the forest, and his face was green with terror. "Look! The trees! They're moving ... they're coming to get us!"

He was right. The trees were moving. Slowly but steadily, the moonlit forest was getting nearer and nearer. Penelope squeaked, Bowser gave an astonished "**YIP!!!**" and Adeline whinnied her amazement.

"Wow!" breathed Alfie. "WOW!"

"I want to go home!" Magnifico's teeth were
chattering with fright. "I don't want to be a hero.
I really, really don't. Please, Alfie … please! Tell this
mangy old nag to turn round, and let's run away very,
very, very fast!"

Adeline snorted indignantly. "Excuse ME, young
fellow. We had an agreement, if you remember. No
personal remarks!"

"Oh, who cares!" The hero had tears of terror
and frustration running down his cheeks. "You
ARE a mangy old nag and I want to go home! I
want to go right now this minute! Alfie, take
me home NOW!"

Alfie didn't answer. He was gradually
realising that it wasn't the forest that was
moving. It was a line of trees and bushes
unlike any trees and bushes he had ever
seen before. They had feet: large hairy feet.
And each pair of feet had twelve toes.

Chapter Ten

"WOOOOEEEEE," Alfie breathed. "Look at that!"

"Nooooooooo…" the hero moaned. "Nooooooo…"

A particularly large bush quivered. The feet stopped moving, the branches dropped, and a hairy figure appeared, a magpie on each shoulder.

"H'mph!" Adeline blew gustily into Alfie's ear. "Spies! I knew those birds were up to no good."

The troll stepped forward. "Greetings to the humbly bodies," he said in a deep growly voice. "I is Rootlie Toot, headly troll of trolls. Black white birdies tells me that hero has come."

Kev looked at Alfie. "Pleased to meet you, I'm sure.

Now, I have a little proposition for you—"

Rootlie Toot interrupted. "I is jibber jabbering
to humbly bodies, not you!"

"What?" Kev was taken
aback. "Beg pardon, I'm sure,
but I need to explain—"

He was interrupted again.
"Birdie! You is too much
word speaking!"

"That's trolls for you,"
Penelope whispered. "They're

very pig-headed. Like the sound of their own voices.
Just as a matter of interest, darling, it's an amazing
honour to meet Rootlie Toot!"

Alfie nodded and asked, "What did he say just
then? I didn't catch it…"

"Actually, dear heart," Penelope said, "he's asking
if the hero will step forward and say a few words."

"Oh dear." Alfie glanced at his brother. Magnifico
was slumped over his picnic baskets, his hands over
his eyes, doing his best to pretend he wasn't there.

"Where is hero?" Rootlie Toot demanded, and as he spoke the rest of the trees and bushes and shrubs dropped their disguise and emerged as a line of short squat trolls, some with two eyes, some with three. All of them had thick matted hair like their leader, and many had long bristly beards. "Headly troll is waiting!" Rootlie Toot stamped his foot.

"Um…" Alfie looked wildly round for help.

"Hat, dear boy!" Adeline hissed. "Take the hat! Pretend to be the hero!"

There didn't seem to be any other choice. Alfie snatched the hat from Magnifico's unresisting head and put it on. Then, with as much of a swagger as he could manage, he stepped forward. "The hero, Magnifico Onion, seventh son of a seventh son, greets you!" He bowed low and Rootlie Toot bowed back, Kev and Perce doing their best to keep their balance.

"Good wordy speak, hero. Seventh son of seventh son is magic humbly body. So will magic humbly body tricksie nasty ogre peoples out of forest?"

Alfie caught the eye of the sleeker magpie, and was astonished to see the bird wink, then nod. *What are those magpies up to?* he wondered.

Rootlie Toot was getting impatient. "Where is word, hero?"

Alfie swallowed. "Erm …
Magnifico Onion wishes to do
… erm … all he can to help."
He paused. Rootlie Toot was
not looking impressed. *Oh well,*
Alfie thought. *I might as well go
for it.* He took a deep breath. "Yes
indeed, Your – Your Trolliness. The
seventh son of the seventh son will
get rid of the ogres. He'll get rid
of the ogres, and find the princess,
and … and win so much gold that
he can live in Glorious Luxury for ever and ever!"

"Awk! Got it in one, laddie!" Kev began a victory
dance on the troll's shoulder. The troll brushed him
off and moved nearer to Alfie.

"So! Humbly bodies like gold and princesseries.
Us trollsies like peacefulness and musherooms.
Trollsies don't like nasty stampy ogres flatting
musherooms and making noise when trollsies want
to shutty star peepers."

Alfie looked blank.

"Sleep, darling," Penelope whispered.

The leader of the trolls bowed again. "Us trollsies will help magic humbly body. Tell us what tricksies you are having in your thinking box to shoo stampy ogres far, far away. Tell us now!" And to Alfie's horror he stood back, hands on hips, and waited for an explanation and a plan.

Alfie's heart was beating so wildly that he could hardly breathe. What should he say? How could he possibly think of any tricks to get rid of the ogres? "Well …" he began, "first of all—"

"Alfie…" It was Magnifico. He had finally dared to peek between his fingers. "ALFIE! Why are you talking to those horrible creatures?"

Rootlie Toot swung round, scowling. "What humbly body is him?"

"That's my brother," Alfie began, but terror had made Magnifico hysterical. He heaved himself up to his full height, his face scarlet and his eyes popping.

"Go away, you revolting things! Go away, I tell you!

Get back to your forest – get back to your oozy woozy swamps and leave us alone! You're ugly and disgusting and—"

"Stop it! Maggers, be quiet!" Alfie yelled, and Adeline threw up her head and rushed at the hero. Grabbing the back of his cloak in her teeth she hurled him into a hazel thicket … but the damage was done. The trolls were growling and muttering to each other, and Rootlie Toot was scowling darkly.

"You is magic hero," he told Alfie, "but brother is badness. BAD badness. Trollsies no help you until badness brother is all gone. Bah!" And with an angry stamp of his foot he marched away.

His band of trolls followed him, but several turned to glare before they went, and a small scrawny troll on the end of the line shook a threatening fist at the space where Magnifico had been. "Us is no ugly! YOU is ugly, humbly body! And you is totally mouldy in your thinking box! So yah!"

Chapter Eleven

THERE WAS A TERRIBLE SILENCE after the trolls had gone.
There was even silence from the hazel thicket.

"He's ruined everything." Alfie was the first to
speak. He was almost crying with frustration. "Those
trolls were going to help us, and Magnifico went and
wrecked it! What are we going to do? How am I ever
going to get him to the castle to kiss the princess?"

"Just a thought, darling…" Penelope sat up on his
shoulder, her whiskers twitching. "Why don't you talk
to those magpies?"

"**Good good good!**" Bowser barked
enthusiastically, and Adeline nodded.

"Clever, dear girl. Very clever."

"Where are they?" Alfie looked round, but there was no sign of the black and white birds. "Hello?" he called. "Magpies? Could I talk to you?"

There was no reply. Bowser jumped forward, and let out a volley of sharp barks.

"Birdies birdies birdies! Oi Oi Oi!"

Hidden in the dense foliage of a holly tree, Perce nudged Kev. "Hey, Kev? Shouldn't we answer?"

"Ssh," Kev said. "I'm thinking."

Perce shook his head. "I thought the troll was our friend. He was ever so pleased when we told him about the hero. And then – bang! Bye bye birdies. There's no trusting trolls, is there, Kev?"

"Perce!" Kev snapped. "Button your beak!"

"No need to be nasty," Perce complained, and he flounced away to the other end of the branch.

Kev went under his wing. He had things to consider.

*   *   *

When it became all too obvious that the birds weren't going to appear, Alfie sighed. "They must have gone. I'd better go and rescue Maggers."

He walked slowly over to the hazel thicket. "Mag— Master!" he called. "Master? Are you all right?"

There was no answer. Not a groan, not a wail, not a mutter.

"Allow me," Penelope said, and she scampered down his arm and dropped to the ground. With a whisk of her white tail she disappeared in-between the gnarled roots, and a moment later there was a startled squeak. "Darling! You'll never guess what – he's vanished!"

"WHAT?" Alfie ran round to the other side, but there was no secret exit, and no sign of his brother. Taking a deep breath, he tried to wriggle into the centre of the thicket, and quickly discovered he could move faster if he crawled on his hands and knees. At first he could feel twigs catching at his hair and his clothes, but then, much to his surprise, his path grew suddenly smooth – exactly as if someone had made it a regular passageway. *Trolls*, Alfie thought, then wished he hadn't. He stretched out an arm to feel ahead of him, and his hand closed round a smooth woody root. Seizing it, he pulled himself forward—

CREAK!!!!!!

"No!" Penelope squeaked, but she was too late. The ground under Alfie had opened. With a jolt he was falling, then sliding down a steep slope …

and rolling and rolling and rolling into complete and utter blackness.

High above him he heard Adeline say, "Dear boy! You seem to have pulled some kind of lever—"

And then he couldn't hear anything for the rush of air in his ears as he slithered down and down and on and on, finally landing with a thump that shook the breath out of his lungs and left him gasping.

"Next time," said a sour little voice, "I suggest you look before you leap. I've no idea where we are, but I suspect it'll be quite impossible to climb back to where we came from." There was a mouse-sized "T'sk! T'sk!" of exasperation. "I don't suppose you have a candle with you, either. This whole expedition suffers from a complete lack of preparation."

Alfie was delighted to discover that he wasn't alone. "Sorry, Norman," he said, and then, "What's that dreadful smell?"

The mouse sniffed, coughed, then sniffed again more cautiously. "Ah," he said.

"What do you mean, 'Ah'?" Alfie asked.

"Ogre," Norman said.

"OGRE?" Alfie gulped. "Is this how they smell?"

The mouse gave a faint chuckle. "They do smell bad, but not as bad as this. I'd say we've landed next to an ogre's rubbish pit. They build them under their houses … and the more the pit smells, the better they like it."

"No wonder the trolls want them out of the forest," Alfie said. "It's making my eyes water. Oh! What's that noise?"

The boy and the mouse listened intently.

"Ooooh … oooooooh … oooooow!"

The moaning came from somewhere in front of them. Alfie got cautiously to his feet and found to his relief that there was room for him to stand. He edged slowly forward, one hand held out into the darkness and the other holding his nose.

"Maggers?" he called. "Are you all right?"

"Of course I'm not!" Magnifico's distant voice was so cross that Alfie breathed a sigh of relief. No one who was seriously hurt could sound so peevish. "I'm bruised from top to toe," the hero went on, "and there's the most disgusting smell, and I can't see anything … but at least we're miles and miles away from those horrible trolls. Get me out of here, and hurry up about it!"

Deciding this was not the moment to mention that they were probably underneath an ogre's house, Alfie worked his way towards the hero. His feet squelched unpleasantly as he walked, and every so often he sank ankle-deep into oozing slime and had to heave himself out. All around him were gurgling noises, and his outstretched hand could feel whiskery spider-web threads floating in front of him, threads that clung to his fingers and filled his nose and mouth. At each step the smell grew worse, until it felt to Alfie as if he was breathing thick greasy fumes rather than air.

And then there was light. Not much … just a wavering yellow light high up above his head, but enough to show him what he was walking through. Bones, rotting skins, mouldering fruit swarming with fat white maggots…

"Yuck," he muttered, and then a shower of snail shells, potato peelings and rotten plums came tumbling down on top of him, almost knocking him over. He staggered to one side, just managing to avoid a torrent of something that might once have been gristle stew but was now green and ghastly.

"All gone," said a loud and echoing voice. "All dinner gone." There was a gusty sigh. "Poor Bilinda, left alone all day long while Dadda and Flugg have fun." There was a pause, and then came the sound of sniffing. "Ho? What is? What is smell?" More sniffing … and a mighty roar that almost deafened Alfie. "HUMAN! Bilinda smells human! Ickle pickle yummy nummy human! Bilinda go find! Go find NOW!" And then he heard the sound of heavy feet crashing away.

Alfie looked wildly round. He and Magnifico had to escape – but where was his brother?

There was still light from above, but he could see no sign of the hero. "Maggers!" he hissed. "Maggers, where are you?"

"Ssssh!" The whispered warning was so close that Alfie jumped. "I'm hiding!"

And a shapeless slimy grey lump at Alfie's feet heaved, sat up, and opened its eyes. "Now get me out! Get me out!"

Chapter Twelve

KEV HAD FINALLY FINISHED THINKING. He stood up on his branch and straightened his tail feathers. "Perce, we're going to talk to the boy!"

"You'll be lucky," Perce said, and Kev stared at him.

"What do you mean?"

Perce looked smug. "He's gone. Told you. Should have answered when he shouted."

"Gone where?" Kev peered through the leaves. "The horse is there. And the mouse and the dog – hey! What's going on? They're all of a tizzy."

While Kev was doing his thinking, Perce had hopped to a higher branch so he could watch what was happening below. "The boy went into that bush to find the hero, and he wasn't there," he reported. "Then the boy was gone too."

"They're hiding," Kev said. "Have to be. People don't just vanish, old buddy."

"They did." Perce was emphatic. "You'd have seen for yourself if you hadn't gone to sleep."

"I was thinking, Perce. Making plans." Kev fluffed out his chest. "Important plans."

"So what are you planning now, Kev?"

Kev made a snap decision. "The castle! That's where we're going. The hero and that boy – I bet they slipped off there while you were looking the other way. And the castle's where the princess is, right? We'll have a snoop around, then when the hero tips up we can tell him what's what. And he'll be grateful, because we'll lead him to his princess so he can live Happily Ever After 'n' all that garbage. So he'll thank us. Generously. And what'll we end up with, Perce?"

Perce opened his beak, but before he could speak Kev added, "And don't you DARE say a word about a nice warm hen's egg!"

Perce looked offended. "I wasn't going to."

"Whatever you say, buddy. But I'll tell you what we're going to end up with. Treasure, Perce, that's what. Twinkly sparkly shiny treasure! So shake those wings. Rosewall Castle, here we come!"

Penelope's eyes were very sharp, and so was her hearing. Kev's voice had risen in his excitement, and she caught the end of his sentence. A moment later she saw the flutter of black and white as the two birds left the holly tree and soared into the night sky. Adeline, following the mouse's gaze, snorted. "Spies! What do you think they're up to?"

The little white mouse twirled a whisker. "They're off to the castle, darling."

"The castle?" Adeline was surprised, and Bowser pricked up his ears.

"Maybe we should go there too," Penelope said

thoughtfully. She twirled a second whisker while she considered. "We don't know where Alfie is, but wherever he is, he'll be with Magnifico … and we know Alfie wants to keep his promise to his Ma. He wants to find a princess for his brother. Where's the princess? In the castle. So sooner or later they'll find their way there."

Adeline looked as if she was about to interrupt, and Penelope held up a paw. "One moment, darling.

Don't forget that Norman's with Alfie, and my brother knows the forest inside out. And if we manage to get there first, we might be able to help – oh!" The mouse stopped. "But I'm so sorry. I'm taking far too much for granted. I'm small and I can hide, and so can Bowser, but you'll be putting yourself in terrible danger, Adeline. Those ogres are huge, fierce and very, very hungry."

"No matter!" Adeline shook her head. "A formal and binding exchange took place, remember. A bag of pork pies went away with J. Jones, and I pledged to follow Alfie Onion through thick and thin, fire and water, hedge and ditch, forest and—"

Penelope nodded. "Thank you, darling. I'm delighted! Now, I suggest we all have a rest. We can start for the castle early in the morning."

"**Sleep sleep sleep**," Bowser said wearily. He had dug hole after hole in an effort to find Alfie and he was exhausted. Adeline whinnied her agreement.

"Time for a snack first," she said. "Might I point out that the hero left his picnics behind? I, of course, will be happy with grass – but it would be a crying shame to let good food go to waste."

"**Woof**," said Bowser. "**Woof woof WOOF!**"

Twenty minutes later, three well-fed animals were fast asleep.

Chapter Thirteen

"WHAT DID YOU SAY?" The slime-covered Magnifico shook with fury. "You FORGOT? You forgot my picnic baskets? But what on earth am I going to eat?"

Alfie sighed. "I didn't know you were going to fall into a tunnel, did I?"

"And that's another thing." The hero glowered. "I've been really, really, REALLY badly treated. That horse threw me! It picked me up and—"

"Maggers!" Alfie waved his arms in front of his brother's face to silence him. "Can you hear footsteps?"

Magnifico was quiet and listened. "Yes," he said uneasily. "Who is it?"

"It's an ogre."

"An ogre?" The hero's voice was a mere whisper.

"And it's coming to look for a yummy nummy human." Norman appeared at the top of Alfie's pocket. "If you ask me, which you haven't, because neither of you have the sense of a woodlouse, you'd best be getting out of here. Fast."

"Ooooooooooooooooh," Magnifico wailed. "I'm going to be eaten!" And he sank down in the slime with his head in his hands.

For a brief moment Alfie considered abandoning his brother to his fate, but his mother's voice echoed in his ears. "Glorious Luxury for every one of us. Even Alfie…" His whole family were relying on him.

"Maggers," he said as firmly as he could, "stand up! We're NOT going to be eaten!" He heaved the wailing hero to his feet. "This way. Get walking!"

"That's better," Norman said approvingly. "But had you thought of climbing rather than walking? The light above us seems to be coming from some kind of rubbish chute. I suspect it was originally a troll escape tunnel, because the intelligent observer will have noticed there are rungs."

Alfie looked up. "You're right … but won't it take us up to the ogre's house?"

"Correct," Norman said. "And where's the ogre?"

"On her way to find us – oh!" Alfie grinned. "I am stupid, aren't I?"

"Yes. Now, if you ask me—"

"We should start climbing." Alfie finished the mouse's sentence for him. "Maggers! Did you hear? We're going to climb up. We're going to escape!"

"No! No no no no NO!" Magnifico clutched at Alfie's arm. "I can't climb up there! Don't make me, Alfie … don't make me!" It was difficult to see the hero's face under its coating of slime and grime, but his cheeks were streaked with tears and his eyes were agonised as he pleaded.

"It'll be fine." Alfie was trying to sound calm, but he was acutely aware that the sound of heavy clomping footsteps was getting nearer and nearer. "Just take it one rung at a time, and you'll be up at the top before you know it!"

"I c-c-c-can't!" Magnifico was wringing his hands and hiccuping with fright. "We can go a different way. I know we can!" And he lurched off into the darkness, his feet squelching hideously at every step. "Come on, Alfie, come on – AAAAAAAAAAAAAAGH!"

Magnifico's scream made Alfie's heart leap in his chest. The silence that followed the scream was almost worse. It seemed to Alfie to last for hours, and then, just as he was despairing of ever seeing his brother again, he heard a voice.

"Don't be frightened, ickle pickle human! Bilinda has you safely in her little net. And you is such a chubbly wubbly thing! Not like those moany bony princes." There was such a loud chuckle that Alfie put his hands to his ears, and as the heavy footsteps began to move away the voice went on, "Bilinda is so happy! Bilinda has her very own ickle pickle human. Going to put you in a cage, ickle pickle ... keep you safe from horrible greedy Dadda and Flugg. Quite safe! And we will play and sing songs, and my chubbly wubbly will be my own dearest pet!"

"Quick!" Norman had scampered out of Alfie's pocket and was sitting on his shoulder. "Now's your chance. Up that ladder!"

"But—" Alfie began, then stopped. There was nothing he could do for Magnifico other than rush after the ogre, and that would mean both of them were caught.

Flinging himself at the rubbish chute, Alfie began to climb, Norman urging him on. Up and up they went, until at last he pulled himself out into

an enormous room lit by flickering lanterns, one of
which was balanced on a splintered wooden table.
He climbed up, and as he looked round he realised he
was in a kitchen … a run-down, peeling, mouldering
kitchen. He was standing not on a table, but on the
draining board of a crazily cracked and chipped
sink full of scummy water and greasy plates. Alfie
shuddered. It reminded him of home, and he hastily
looked away – and found himself staring straight into
the pages of a huge cookbook propped open at the end
of the draining board.

"*Princes Pie*," he read. "*A powerful spell and a delicious treat.*"

He crawled closer.

"*One: Take seven fresh princes, one hundred per cent royal, and chop small.*

Two —"

"What are you doing?" Norman was tugging at Alfie's ear.

But Alfie didn't move. He read on, "*Two: Fill a saucepan of sufficient size with oak root and lavender.*

Three: Mix all together, heat and stir."

Fascinated, Alfie turned back a page. "*This spell brings boldness and the appearance of a handsome prince.*" Alfie froze, then read the page again. "A handsome prince…" he muttered, and rubbed his nose. "The ogre wants to look like a handsome prince … but why?"

"ALFIE ONION!" Norman was beside himself as he danced up and down on Alfie's shoulder. "She's here! You've got to hide!"

At last Alfie heard. Blinking, he jumped off the draining board and onto the floor. The kitchen was full of cupboards of all shapes and sizes – choosing one at random Alfie pulled the door open.

"A prison?" Alfie shook his head and looked again. Behind the door were strong steel bars, and he was almost sure that he could see a body lying on the floor in the gloom. "Hello?" he whispered.

There was no answer other than a faint snore.

The kitchen door handle rattled and Alfie gasped, slid into the cupboard, and pulled the door shut. The bars pressed painfully into his back, and he wondered how long it would be before he was forced to move. Heavy footsteps were crossing the kitchen floor. He held his breath.

"Ickle pickle chubbly one, don't be scared! Bilinda won't eat you. And Bilinda won't let mean old Flugg and Dadda eat you. Bilinda hates mean old Flugg! He gets everything … but he hasn't got an ickle pickle … so boo to mean old Flugg, because you is mine. All mine!" There was the sound of banging and crashing as if a pile of furniture was being moved, and Bilinda went on, "Look! See this pretty cage?

My ickle pickle will be safe in here. Don't be sad, ickle pickle. Bilinda makes yummy sweeties. Do you like chocolate, chubbly one? See this nice big strawberry cream? Half for Bilinda, and half for ickle you … no, no – say please! No snatching!"

Alfie held his breath. Would Magnifico answer?

"Oh, whatever," said a familiar voice. "Please, then, if you insist."

The ogre gave a delighted chuckle. "Oh, lovely chubbly wubbly! Look how he slobbers and gobbles! Here … have more!"

Alfie couldn't bear it any longer. He pushed the cupboard door open a fraction, and peered out. His brother was sitting in an old-fashioned wire birdcage, and the ogre was kneeling beside him, feeding him from the most enormous bag of sweets that Alfie had ever seen. All that was recognisable of the hero was his eyes; he was caked in greenish-grey slime from top to toe, and every so often Bilinda leant forward and gave him an appreciative sniff. "Yummy! Ickle pickle smells so yummy!

Bilinda LOVES her chubbly wubbly."

To Alfie's surprise, Bilinda wasn't ugly. She was nearly twice as tall as he was, and solidly built, but she had pink cheeks and bright blue eyes.

"Ickle pickle," she said, as she poked yet another chocolate through the bars, "don't be greedy. You is gobble gobbling too much! Too much sweeties bad for you. Does my ickle pickle like … sausage?"

"Sausage?" Magnifico jumped off his perch. "I love sausages! Give me a sausage!"

Bilinda drew back frowning, and shook a huge finger at the hero. "Naughty ickle pickle! What does pickle have to say to nice kind Bilinda?"

Magnifico rattled the bars of his cage. "I don't care! I want sausages! I'm STARVING!"

The ogre shook her head sadly. "No no no, ickle pickle." She picked up a filthy dishcloth and draped it over the cage. "You sit under there quiet and think. Bilinda must teach you to be good and polite and nice." She yawned, showing very white teeth that were also very sharp. "Bilinda tired. Going to go to beddie byes. Come along, ickle pickle. Sausage in the morning, if you be good and ask nicely!"

And picking up the cage in one hand and a lantern in the other, the ogre stomped out of the kitchen.

Chapter Fourteen

ALFIE WAITED UNTIL THE FOOTSTEPS had died away before he opened his cupboard and crawled out.

"Norman, that recipe! It's a spell! To make you as handsome as a prince. And it needs seven princes – all chopped up! But why does the ogre want to be handsome?"

Norman tutted impatiently. "Think, boy! Think! What are all the princes after? And your brother, come to that."

"Oh!" As light dawned, Alfie's eyes widened. "The ogre wants to kiss the princess, and get the gold and the castle!"

"It's as plain as the rather ordinary nose on your rather ordinary face," Norman said. "But I'm guessing the ogre's planning it for his son." He twirled a whisker. "I think I'd better go and see what's happening in the rest of the house…"

As Norman scampered away, Alfie cautiously tiptoed to a chair. From the chair he climbed onto the draining board, collected the lantern and took it back with him to the cupboard. The yellow light chased the shadows away, and he saw several bodies lying on heaps of grubby satin cushions. All of them wore silk or velvet, and in one corner was a pile of gleaming crowns. In another corner was a blackened saucepan, some dubious-looking bottles and a heap of dirty bowls, and there was a sickly sweet smell hanging in the air. He opened the cupboard door wider and inspected the prisoners.

Princes, he thought. *They must be the princes the ogres were knocking on the head ... they're being kept here for the pie to make the spell!*

He gave the bars a shake, but they were solid. Leaning forward he gave a low whistle, but none of the sleepers stirred.

"The ogre's given them some kind of sleeping potion," Alfie decided. He whistled again, and the nearest prince gave a faint moan and opened heavy eyes. He stared unseeingly at Alfie.

"Woop ... woop ... pass the teapot..."

"Who are you?" Alfie asked.

The prince's sleepy gaze sharpened a little. "I know what ... you are. You're a nasty ... nasty troll. Go ... go away."

"I'm not a troll," Alfie said indignantly. "I'm a boy!"

"They warned ... they warned us ... nasty little trolls come up the troll hole..." The prince attempted to lift a hand. "But ... but we're safe ... safe ... safe ... in here. Flugg locked us away ... ex ... excellent chap..." His voice trailed off, and his eyes closed.

"Wake up!" Alfie hissed. "Wake up! You're in serious danger! You've got to understand – the ogres want to make you into a pie!"

"No … no…" The prince rolled his head from side to side as a foolish smile crossed his face. "Quite … quite wrong, my dear old … dear old beanio…"

"No!" Alfie pulled at the bars. "It's true, I tell you. You're going to be made into Princes Pie! I've seen the recipe! The ogres want to make a spell!"

One bleary eye unwillingly opened. "My dear old bean … you're barking mad. Pie … super dooper pie … is for our … celebration. Yes … Princes Pie! Pie for me … and pie for Boodles…"

The eye closed, the prince rolled away, and all Alfie could hear was the sound of heavy snoring. He sighed and picked up the lamp.

"Excuse me … I say! Peasant!" Alfie spun round and saw a small white hand waving at him through the bars. "I'm ever so sorry to be a nuisance, but if it's not too much trouble could you possibly let me out?" A peaky face topped with floppy hair and a lopsided golden crown loomed into the glow of Alfie's light. "I'm Prince Rufus. Couldn't help hearing what you were saying to Jules," the prince lowered his voice, "about the *pie!*"

"It's true," Alfie said.

The prince began to tremble. "But mummy will be ever so cross if I'm popped in a pie!" He clasped his hands together. "I just knew that horrid ogre was telling fibs, saying he was going to cook us a special treat. But Jules and Boodles and the others would keep drinking his horrible snail and poppy soup and they wouldn't listen. PLEASE rescue me!"

Alfie was studying the bars. They were held in place with four large padlocks. "Have you seen the keys anywhere?"

"Can't you bend them?" Rufus looked astonished. "Mummy always says peasants are quite tremendously strong. All that fresh air and chopping turnips!"

"I'm not a peasant." Alfie frowned. "I'm a boy – and I need keys."

Rufus was already wandering away, his shoulders drooping. "Mummy's going to be so cross … so cross…" He kicked moodily at one of the bottles and it fell over and cracked. An ooze of green liquid spread across the floor, and the sickly sweet smell doubled and trebled in strength. "Ooooomph," said the prince as he sank to his knees. "Oooooo … mph!" And he fell over, fast asleep.

Alfie could feel his own eyelids growing heavy and his brain growing numb. He backed away hastily, shaking his head and rubbing at his eyes.

"Pssssst!" Norman was beckoning him from the other side of the kitchen. Alfie slammed the cupboard door shut and ran across.

"What is it?" he asked.

"Time to go," Norman said. "That ogre girl's fast asleep, and so's the hero. He's snoring his head off on a heap of feathers … not a care in the world. And you might like to know that there are bags and bags of gold in the hallway. Fancy helping yourself?"

Alfie was horrified. "No! That's stealing!"

The mouse sniffed. "And you think the ogres worked for it? You're even greener than I thought, Alfie Onion. That'll be stolen gold, sure as eggs is eggs. Ogres can never get enough of the stuff. They always want more and more."

"I can't…" Alfie began, but Norman saved him his explanation.

"Maybe best to leave it for now. Heavy stuff, gold – it'll slow you down, and you need to hurry."

"Hurry?" Alfie asked. His long day had caught up with him, and he was very, very tired.

The mouse waved a paw. "Didn't you count those princes? Six of them lying around in that cage, and the recipe calls for seven. So the ogres only need one more, and then it'll be Pie Time! And who knows what nincompoop of a prince might be wandering through the forest at this very moment, all ready to be bopped on the head."

Alfie stifled a yawn. "Oh … yes."

"Come along, then. The front door's got bars and chains, but there's a window you can climb through. Once we're out of here we can head for the castle." The mouse nodded knowingly. "And I'll bet you a slice of cheese to a peanut we'll find my sister there waiting for us."

Alfie looked startled. "But I can't leave here without Maggers! And what about the princes?"

"Why can't you?" Norman sat up and fixed Alfie with a stern gaze. "The princes and your brother are safe for now, especially your brother. You heard that ogre. He's her ickle pickle chubbly wubbly pet. And you can travel much faster without him trailing along."

"I don't understand," Alfie said. "What's the point of me going to the castle on my own? It's Maggers who's got to kiss the princess! He's the hero."

"Give me strength!" Norman rolled his eyes. "Think, boy, think! You've got to get rid of the ogres before there's even the faintest chance of any kissing! Get rid of them – and the rest is easy."

Remembering how big Bilinda was, Alfie felt giant butterflies swirl in his stomach. How big would her brother be? Let alone her father? But Norman was right.

"We'll head for the castle," he said. "Let's go."

Chapter Fifteen

THE MAGPIES CIRCLED the castle battlements as the early morning sun was just beginning to break through the clouds. Perce landed on a turret and looked round. "Nice view! You can see right over the forest."

Kev came to perch beside him. "We're not here to look at the view, buddy. Got to check out the scene." He peered downwards and whistled. "Ogres ahoy! Big ogres, too!"

"Awk!" Perce wobbled for a moment as he took in the size of the two figures slumped below. Wild thorny roses surrounded the castle as far as the eye could see, but a crooked pathway had been trampled through, and between the gates and the main entrance where the ogres lay nothing was left but broken stems and crushed petals and leaves. "They're GIGANTIC," Perce said. "And ever so ugly. And hairy. Hairy and scary."

Perce was right. The ogres had bristling eyebrows, and enormous noses covered in whiskers and warts. They appeared to be asleep, but the younger one's eyelids flickered, his huge hairy toes twitched, and every so often he shivered.

Kev watched with his head on one side. "Looks like that one's having a bad dream. Serves him right."

"What's an ogre scared of, Kev?" Perce asked. "If I was that big I wouldn't be scared of anything."

Kev scratched his neck. "You've got a point. H'm. Think I'll have a quick squiz the other way."

He stretched his wings and flew to the other side of the battlements, leaving Perce studying the ogres.

"Awk?" he said, by way of experiment. "AWK?"

The younger ogre opened his eyes, looked up – and leapt to his feet, roaring, "AAAAAGH!"

Perce was so surprised he fell off his turret, saving himself with wild flutterings.

"AAAAAAGH!" The ogre shook his father awake and pointed at Perce. "AAAAAAAAGH!"

The magpie decided it was time to remove himself from view. He scrambled away as a deep voice boomed, "Flugg! Stupid Flugg!"

"But Dadda—" Flugg's voice was squeakier than his father's, and younger than Perce had expected— "Dadda I saw a bad sign! A bad sign black and white bird! It means bad bad things, Dadda!"

"Rubbish." The older ogre was angry. "You talk rubbish, Flugg! There is no bad bird, no bad sign. Lie down and sleep." He yawned, and rolled over.

Flugg, huge as he was, began to grizzle. "Can't sleep, Dadda. Want to go home…"

His father grunted. "One more prince and all is good. GOOD, do you hear? One prince and six princes is seven for pie! Special Princes Pie for Flugg, to make him bold and handsome!"

But Flugg wasn't interested in pie. He was walking to and fro, staring up at the battlements and muttering to himself, "Bad bad bird…"

On an inspiration, Perce popped his head out, waved a wing and disappeared again. He was thrilled to hear a wail of terror from down below.

"What's going on?" Kev had flown back. Perce, first checking that neither of them could be seen, explained. "Wooooeee!" Kev looked at Perce with something approaching admiration. "Ogres are scared of magpies! COOL!"

Perce shook his head. "Only the young one." He gave a small smug cough. "I'm a terrible bad sign!"

"Excellent!" Kev jumped happily from foot to foot. "Keep it going, Perce! Pop up and down and keep him twitchy, buddy. There's an interesting chimney I want to check…" And he was gone.

"Kev thought I was clever," Perce told himself proudly. "Nobody's ever said that before. Awk!"

He celebrated by making another brief appearance on a different turret, and was rewarded by yet another agonised howl from Flugg. He was so delighted that he flew a triumphant loop … and just missed being hit by a well-aimed rock.

"GET AWAY, BIRD!" Flugg's father was picking up a second rock, a fierce look on his whiskery face.

"Ooops!" Perce retired behind a flagpole.

Kev was inspecting a chimney on the far side of the castle. He had noticed a thin wisp of smoke rising into the early morning sky when he and Perce arrived, and although there was now no sign of it he was intrigued.

Someone's in there, he thought, and he hopped round the pot, listening. Was someone singing? He couldn't be sure. With an "Ak ak ak" of irritation he flew across to a tall pine tree to have a better view of the castle windows.

"Shoo! Get away, you thief! I know your kind, and we don't want you here. Shoo!" A large pigeon was flapping her wings and trying to push Kev off his branch. "Shoo, I said! SHOO!"

"My dear lady," Kev began, but the pigeon was determined to get rid of him.

"Don't you go my dear ladying me! As if we don't have enough to deal with, what with ogres stomping about making a mess and scaring my chicks and making that poor girl's life a misery. So be off with you! Shoo!"

Deciding there was no point in arguing, Kev flew back to the castle. It was only as he landed that he realised what the pigeon had said. A girl! Might it be a princess? A princess singing inside the castle? Kev put his head on one side and shut his eyes in order to concentrate.

Perce fluttered over to join him. "Got a headache, Kev?" he asked tenderly.

"No!" Kev snapped. "I'm trying to listen."

"OK," Perce said. "Did you see the boy?"

Kev opened his eyes. "What boy? Where?"

"Over there, look. Coming this way. The one we saw with the hero, Kev. But the hero's not there. Just the boy ... and a mouse. Oh – and there's a lady ogre carrying a cage on the other side of the trees."

Chapter Sixteen

IT WAS LUCKY FOR ALFIE that Bilinda chose that moment to burst into song.

"La la la la!" she carolled. "Bilinda is ever so ever so happy! Not lonely no more!"

Alfie, seeing a large hollow tree, scrambled inside as fast as he could. "How close is she?" he whispered. "Do you think she saw us?"

Norman, dozing in Alfie's pocket, had woken with a start. After listening for a moment he shook his head. "Far enough." He paused. "She'd smell you before she saw you. Bad eyesight, excellent sense of smell. Talking of which, might I recommend a wash when you have the opportunity? We're heading for a castle, remember. It's just possible that you might meet a princess, and there's an unfortunate whiff of sewage about you that she might not appreciate."

There was no answer. The hollow tree was warm, the leaves were soft, and Alfie hadn't slept for a very long time. Norman gave an irritated sniff and scampered out of his pocket so he could pull the boy's hair.

Alfie stirred, but didn't wake. "I'll do the washing up in a minute, Ma," he murmured, then sank back into his dreams. Norman tutted angrily and ran to peer out of the tree. There was no sign of Bilinda, but he could still hear her; she was chatting happily about sausages and chocolates and ickle pickle darlings.

Curiosity overcame caution. Norman scrambled out of his hiding place, leaving Alfie snoring gently. The mouse slipped in and out of the undergrowth until he found a beech tree with low-lying branches. With a twirl of his tail he climbed until he had a clear view.

Bilinda was stomping along a well-trodden path that led to the gap her father and brother had made in the thorns surrounding the castle. Her birdcage was in one hand and a large canvas bag was in the other. Norman could see Magnifico sitting in the cage; he was still covered in grey slime but it had dried and was beginning to flake off. It did not improve his appearance, but Bilinda seemed even more devoted than she had been the night before. She cooed and murmured to her prisoner, and every so often she put the cage down so she could give him a treat from her bulging pockets. Magnifico accepted these offerings with enthusiasm and, much to Norman's astonishment, sounded grateful.

"Ta," he said, and Bilinda clapped her hands.

"Such a poppetty darling! He's Bilinda's bestest sweetie! And what would chubbly wubbly like next?"

"Sausages," said the chubbly wubbly, "please."

Norman nearly fell off his branch.

* * *

"DAUGHTER!" The ogre's shout made the trees quiver. "DAUGHTER! Where's my food? Grindbone is HUNGRY!"

Bilinda's face lost its beaming smile. She hid Magnifico's cage in a clump of bracken, and scurried forward clutching the bag.

"Here, Dadda."

Her father came marching towards her, his hand outstretched. "Give! You is USELESS girl! You is LATE!" Snatching the bag, he slapped Bilinda so hard she reeled backwards. "LAZY! Why you late?"

Flugg appeared behind his father, scowling heavily. "Where my sausages, stupid?" He tried to grab the bag from his father and a tussle took place, each trying to be the first to pull out the sausages. When they finally managed to heave out a couple of long strings they stuffed them into their mouths with their enormous hands, snuffling and dribbling as they did so.

"What next?" Flugg demanded. He dived back
into the bag, and pulled out a lump of burnt bread.
"RUBBISH!" He hurled it at Bilinda, and searched
again. A chunk of raw meat proved more satisfactory,
and he tore at it with a grim determination, glaring

at his sister all the while. "When I King of Castle," he said, "you will be nowhere, stupid Bilinda. You will be gone! Flugg will have pretty princess to make food for him … not stupid lazy ogre girl like you!" And he began to crack the bone with his strong yellowed teeth.

Up on the roof Kev clicked his beak in surprise. "Hey, Perce! Hear that? The ogre's after the princess! AND the castle!"

Bilinda glared back at her hideous brother. "You is wrong, Flugg! Dadda will let Bilinda stay in castle too!" Her voice was not as confident as her words, and she gave her father an anxious glance. "Is so, Dadda?"

Her father wheeled round, and slapped her a second time, this time so hard he knocked her over.

"Stupid! Flugg not want you! Grindbone not want you. Grindbone never want you – you is useless girl. NOBODY want you when Flugg King of Castle!" He heaved the bag away from his son, pulled out a handful of cold meat pies and crammed them into his mouth, talking all the time and spitting crumbs in all directions. "Pretty princess will see Bilinda and say UGLY UGLY UGLY, so Bilinda must go way for ever ever EVER…" He stopped, and began to sniff the air. "What? What what WHAT? Does I smell human?"

Bilinda, tears rolling down her cheeks, sat up. "No, Dadda! Not human! Is … is yummy pie that Bilinda made for Dadda and Flugg." Her voice was growing more and more desperate. "Look in bag, Dadda. See yummy pie, Dadda! Look in bag!"

Her father ignored her. Piggy little eyes half-closed, he was sniffing from left to right and up and down. "Is human," he muttered. "I smell human. Grindbone's nose never wrong. Is prince? Prince for pie … but where? WHERE?" With a grunt he focused his gaze on the path Bilinda had just hurried down. "Is there.

Human is there." And he began lumbering towards the bracken where the cage was hidden, Flugg at his heels.

"NO, Dadda!" Bilinda screamed, and she clutched at her father's ragged trousers as he passed her. "Is my dearest chubbly wubbly and I found him and is mine! Isn't prince! Is ickle pickle! Is MINE!"

She was too late. Her father had found the cage, and Magnifico's piercing shriek of terror shocked the two magpies on the castle roof.

"Get ready for action, Perce," Kev warned. "Can't quite see who's down there in that cage. Just a minute … wowsers! It's the hero! And the ogre's shaking the cage to get him out – and the ogre girl's on her knees crying her eyes out – and her brother's trying to kick her out of the way."

Perce blinked. "That's not very nice, Kev," he said. "That's not nice at all."

"Certainly isn't," Kev agreed. "Right! Magpie deployment! We'll give him some Terrible Bad Luck…" And with a loud "Akakakakakakak", he swooped down and circled above the ogres' heads.

"AAAGH!" Covering his hairy head with his hands, Flugg abandoned his weeping sister and rushed for the castle as fast as his heavy legs would carry him. "Bad! BAD!" he yelled, and hurled himself into the thickest of the thorns at the bottom of the tower.

Grindbone, taken by surprise, dropped the cage and Bilinda flung herself on top of it, cuddling the bars and trying to soothe the terrified Magnifico.

For a moment the enormous ogre stood still, staring blankly after his son. In the distance a horse whinnied … and the ogre's face brightened. "PRINCE!"

Looking first at the cage, and then away beyond the castle, Grindbone tried to think what to do next. "Catch prince…" he decided. "Prince for pie!" He rubbed his enormous hairy hands together and chuckled as he considered the future. "First prince, then pie, then princess, then castle, then gold! Ha!"

Bending down, he caught the sobbing Bilinda by the arm and jerked her to her feet. "Go!" he ordered.

"Put human in cupboard with princes." He licked
his red rubbery lips, and patted his bulging stomach.
"Will eat with pie." A thought came to him,
and he heaved a jangling bunch of keys
out of his pocket. "Put in cage and give

poppy snail soup. Keep quiet …
keep sleepy." Shaking his
daughter ferociously to
make sure she understood,
he grinned a hideous
broken-toothed grin. "No trickeries,
mind! If human not in cupboard, Dadda will eat YOU,
Bilinda!" He gave the girl ogre one last violent shake,
then flung her into the bracken and marched off to the
castle. His daughter crawled to the cage and peered
inside.

"Is all right, ickle pickle dearest," she whispered.
"Bilinda will run away with chubbly wubbly. Bilinda
promises will keep ickle pickle safe safe safe!"

Chapter Seventeen

ALFIE HAD HEARD HIS BROTHER'S SCREAM in his sleep, and it had become part of a nightmare full of wriggling white maggots and faceless figures buried in heaps of feathers. He woke with a start; someone was pulling his nose.

Brushing leaves away from his face, Alfie sat up and saw the small scrawny troll who had shaken his fist when Magnifico upset Rootlie Toot.

"Hello," Alfie said. "Erm … how do you do?"

The little troll shook his head. "No time for jibber jabber. You is here to tricksie Grindbone and Flugg?"

Alfie hesitated. "Yes?"

"Good!" The troll nodded his approval. "Rootlie Toot smiley all over! He hear badness brother shut in cage – he say, 'Ha! Good catching! Now hero can tricksie ogres!' Will go tell Rootlie Toot all is true."

And the troll was gone.

"Norman?" Alfie sat up straight and looked round for the mouse. "Have I been asleep long? Norman, where are you?" Not wanting to raise his voice above a whisper, he gave a low whistle.

"Oi!" An outraged Norman came scampering towards him. "What's with the whistle?"

"Sorry," Alfie apologised. "I didn't know where

you'd gone. Have I been asleep for ages? I've just seen a troll! What's going on?"

Norman gave a sour chuckle. "You've managed to sleep through your brother being caught by the ogres at the castle."

"WHAT?"

The mouse twirled a whisker. "No worries. He hasn't been eaten yet. He's with the girl ogre, and she's feeding him chocolate to soothe his nerves. Then she wants them to run away together." Norman sniffed. "There's no accounting for taste. He's that way." He pointed towards the path.

Forgetting that he might be putting himself in serious danger, Alfie jumped out of the hollow tree and dashed in the direction Norman had shown him. His progress was hardly silent, but Bilinda, bending tenderly over the birdcage, didn't hear him or see him until he was standing right beside her.

"Let my brother go!" Alfie shouted. "Please … PLEASE let him go!"

Bilinda sat back and stared in astonishment, her blue eyes very wide. "Is another human!"

"Alfie?" Magnifico was sitting on his perch, his mouth smeared with chocolate. "Where have you been? I was attacked by an ogre. He swung me in the air. He wanted to eat me." His frown grew fiercer. "Ma said you were to look after me! YOU were meant to be eaten first, and it was nearly ME!"

"Will be no eating, ickle pickle," Bilinda said. Her face was badly bruised and wet with tears, but she was doing her best to smile. "Bilinda promises."

"Good," Magnifico gave a regal nod, then glanced at Alfie to see if he was listening. "See? YOU don't look after me, but Bilinda does."

But Alfie's attention was elsewhere. He had seen the bunch of keys lying in the bracken, and his heart was beginning to race. He took a deep breath, and looked up at the ogre. "Are those the keys to the cage? The cage in the cupboard in your house?"

"Not ever going to house again," Bilinda told him. "Am running away from mean horrid Dadda and mean horrid Flugg ... never going back. Never!"

Alfie's head was whirling. If he had the keys he could release the princes, and there would be no Princes Pie. But surely the most important thing was to get the ogres out of the way? If he didn't, there was no way Magnifico could kiss the princess. Could he somehow lead the ogres away from the castle? Was there some way they could be distracted? If he waited till night, could he and Magnifico tiptoe past their huge sleeping bodies? But DID ogres sleep?

And then it came to him. The sleeping potion! The sleeping potion that Grindbone had given the princes. If the ogres were drugged, he could sneak Magnifico into the castle to kiss the princess...

But how could he get hold of the potion? And would it work on the ogres? If it did, and he and Magnifico reached the princess safely, what would happen next? Would the fact that the hero had won his princess be enough to send the ogres running away? That was how one of his mother's fairy tales ended ... but would Grindbone and Flugg know that was the expected behaviour?

Alfie heaved a massive sigh. All he could do was take the risk. The keys were lying beside him, and in front of him was a large girl ogre who was cooing at his brother. It was time for action.

Alfie bowed. "Excuse me, ma'am," he said. "Would you ... that is, might you like to help me? Me and the – erm – ickle pickle?"

Bilinda wiped her face with the edge of her grubby apron, leaving smears on her cheeks. "Help?" she repeated. "Help do what?"

"I want to set the princes free," Alfie explained, "and collect some of those bottles.

Snail soup? Is that what's in them? I need it so ...
so we can try to get inside the castle."

He felt it would be a step too far to explain that
he wanted to drug her father and brother, but Bilinda
surprised him.

"Poppy snail soup for Dadda and Flugg?" she asked, and a conspiratorial smile slowly spread across her face. "Oh yes. Poppy snail soup make them sleep. Sleep good!" She paused. "Why you need get in?"

Alfie pointed at the cage. "Magnifico – the ickle pickle – is the seventh son of a seventh son, and that's very special. Very special indeed! That makes him a hero! That's why he's here in the forest: he's adventuring. Going to find his fortune, like in the fairytale book. He has to get into the castle so he can kiss the princess, and then he'll live Happily Ever After, with lots and lots of gold and…"

Alfie's voice died away. Bilinda had sunk to her knees, her shoulders shaking with silent sobs. She looked so unhappy that Alfie found himself running to hug as much of her as he could reach.

"I'm sorry," he said. "I'm so sorry – what is it? What did I say?"

The girl pushed him away, her eyes swimming with tears. "Ickle pickle will go with princess?"

"Erm … yes," Alfie said. "Yes, I suppose he will.

My family are hoping he'll bring them enough gold to live in Glorious Luxury for ever and ever, you see…"

Bilinda drooped even more, and the sobs came faster. "Ickle pickle has family?"

"There's Ma, and Pa, and six brothers as well as me," Alfie told her. Every word he said seemed to make the girl more miserable, and he was feeling worse and worse.

"So ickle pickle not go away with Bilinda…" The ogre threw herself on her face and began to cry as if her heart was torn in pieces. "Oh, lonely Bilinda! Lonely, lonely, LONELY Bilinda…"

"OI! Listen to me!" Magnifico was banging on the bars of his cage. "You can come home with us if you want. I don't mind. Just don't cry! I hate crying."

The tears stopped, and Bilinda slowly sat up, gazing at Magnifico as if he were the most precious thing in the whole wide world. "Go with darling chubbly wubbly?"

"Yes." The hero shrugged. "Like I said, I don't mind. Tell her, Alfie."

Alfie blinked in astonishment. What on earth would his mother and father say? Maybe it was best not to think too far into the future.

"Yes," he said. "Come home with us!"

At once Bilinda wiped away her tears. "Bilinda help. Bilinda fetch poppy snail soup."

"Thank you," Alfie said. "And you'll let the princes out?"

The girl ogre nodded. "Let moany princes out." She pocketed the keys and picked up the birdcage. "Come, ickle pickle. Come with Bilinda—"

"Oh!" Alfie hadn't expected this. "Erm … wouldn't it be quicker if you left Maggers – the ickle pickle – here?"

"NO WAY!" A mutinous expression that Alfie knew all too well had settled on the ickle pickle's face. "I'm not going to stay here. It's not safe."

Alfie stared at his brother. He seemed perfectly happy to be sitting in a cage carried by an ogre who was more than twice his size. Indeed, he had the air of a king riding in a carriage.

"I want to go with Bilinda," the hero went on. "SHE looks after me!"

Bilinda gave a coo of pleasure. "Darling precious little chubbly!" She put her head on one side and blew kisses at him. "Like to ride on Bilinda's shoulder?"

Magnifico shook his head. "I want some bars between me and the horrible forest!"

Bilinda patted the cage. "Bilinda will keep you safe, chubbly wubbly. You is my dearest darling!" And she strode away, the birdcage in her arms.

Chapter Eighteen

"WAIT!" Norman was running through the leaves. "Wait!"

Alfie swung round. "Hi, Norman!"

"What have you done?" The mouse was incandescent with rage. "Do you really think you'll ever see her or your brother again?"

"Yes," Alfie said. "Yes, I do."

"Then you're as stupid as the ogres," Norman snapped. "You mark my words, you'll live to be sorry you're so trusting."

"Awk?"

Norman and Alfie jumped. Kev had flown silently

down and was perched above their heads, studying them with interest. "Bit of a barney? Bit of a ruckus? Me and Perce, we do it all the time!"

Alfie peered at the black and white bird. "Hey! It was you who told the trolls a hero was coming to the forest, wasn't it?"

Kev shrugged. "Good plan, went wrong," he said. "Not our fault, if you don't mind my saying so. And those ogres are after the princess, same as your hero. Want to get their hands on the gold."

"I know that," Alfie said. "Erm ... are you two spies? Or what?"

"Hang about!" Kev gave him a reproachful look. "Who was that who got hairy scary Flugg running for cover just now? Me and Perce, that's who!"

Alfie looked at Norman for confirmation, and the mouse nodded. "It would appear Flugg is superstitious," he said. "One magpie, and he was off."

"Dived into the rose bushes," Kev said cheerfully.

"He was sitting picking thorns out of his knees a moment ago. The big one's standing guard with the knobbliest club you ever did see. Thinks there's a prince about to come riding up because he heard a horse whinny. Going to be dead disappointed when he finds out it's your team!"

"My team? You mean Adeline and Bowser and Penelope?" An anxious expression crossed Alfie's face. "Where were they? Are they near here?"

The bird put his head on one side. "Not far, as it happens. Not far. But I'd like an answer myself. Perce and me – we're useful. Very useful. So if we're useful to you, what's in it for us?"

Norman sniffed. "I don't imagine you'd think it was enough reward simply to do a good deed?"

"Nah." Kev shook his head, then added, "Didn't care to see that ogre beating up his girl, mind. Not good, that."

"What would you like?" Alfie asked. "I haven't got anything much. We'll have more when Maggers has kissed the princess, though."

The magpie's eyes gleamed. "Any chance of some twinkly sparkly shiny stuff?"

"If we find any, it's yours," Alfie promised.

"Done deal." The magpie winked. "The mouse can bear witness."

"Me? I disapprove of the whole arrangement," Norman said stiffly. "If you ask me, this young man is making one bad decision after another. First—"

Norman's rant was interrupted by a rustling in the bracken, and a moment later Bowser was leaping up at Alfie and covering him with wet doggy kisses.

"BOWSER!" Alfie was overjoyed. "I've missed you so much! Where are Adeline and Penelope?"

"**Near near near!**" Bowser panted. "**Come come come!**" His eyes fell on Kev. "**Who he?**"

"It's OK," Alfie said. "He's a friend. He's going to help us … but let's go and find the others! Norman, do you want to go back in my pocket?"

The mouse gave an exaggerated sigh. "If it's not too much trouble. I'd hoped I might be considered as a friend, but evidently not. You prefer the company of ogres and birds of fancy plumage."

Alfie smiled as he picked the mouse up. "You've been an amazing friend, Norman."

"H'mph," the mouse said, but he settled himself comfortably in Alfie's pocket with no further complaint.

Bowser was looking puzzled. "**Where where where hero?**"

"Long story – I'll tell you when I tell the others," Alfie said. He looked at Kev. "Could you see how Bilinda and Magnifico are getting on? Please? I don't know how long we've got before they get back."

"No probs," the magpie said. "Perce is on watch for ogre action. Ak ak ak! You'd better meet him."

He called again, and a flutter of black and white came flying down from the castle tower. A distant roar followed, and Perce landed beside Kev looking pleased with himself.

"Hear that?" he said proudly. "That's me! I'm a Bad Bird! Makes that ogre yell every time!"

Kev nudged him. "Ssh! Look, the lad here, he and I've done a deal. We're on his side. Got it? You get back up to that tower and keep your peepers open – no dozing. Any sign of ogre attack, you fly straight to young Alfie and report. Understand?"

Perce shifted from foot to foot. "Um … might there be a nice warm hen's egg at the end of all this?"

"If we find one, it's yours," Alfie said. "Oh, and lots of twinkly – what was it?"

"Twinkly sparkly shiny stuff," Kev prompted.

"Yes. That too. I promise."

"Can't say fairer than that, can he, Perce?" Kev gave his partner a push. "Off you go, old buddy of mine!" He stretched his wings. "Be seeing you…"

As Kev left in one direction and Perce in the other, Bowser led Alfie down a narrow winding path. "**Ssh ssh ssh!**" he warned. "**Too too too near ogres!**"

Alfie did his best to move as silently as he could. After a short while he realised they were circling the castle; there were towering banks of tangled roses all along one side of the path that they were following, and the shuttered windows looked down on him. Alfie wondered about the princess asleep inside. What would she be like? What would happen after Magnifico kissed her? Would she be pleased? What if she wasn't?

"You're thinking too much, dear boy," said Adeline's familiar voice. "I can tell!"

Alfie glanced up and saw the horse right in front of him. Penelope was dancing up and down on her saddle in a state of huge excitement. "Darling!" she trilled. "How wonderful to see you! Where's the hero?"

Norman had scampered out of Alfie's pocket and onto his shoulder. "Lost for ever," he announced. "Hello, Penelope. This young man's gone mad. I did my best to advise him, but he wouldn't listen.

Penelope smiled at Alfie. "Mad? Are you mad, darling? What have you done?"

"Well…" Alfie began his story, and the horse, the dog and the mouse listened intently. When he got to the end, Norman shook his head.

"Mad. Stark, staring mad. We'll never ever see his brother again. It's a fine sort of adventuring when you lose the hero!"

His sister sighed. "You always think the worst, ducky. Bilinda never hurt us, did she? All she did was wander round singing sad songs. It was her father and brother who ruined our house."

Norman refused to be convinced. "When we're still sitting here waiting in three days' time, you'll wish you'd listened to me."

"She'll come back," Alfie said. "I know she will."

Bowser sat up. "**Back back back!**" he barked, and Alfie gave him a hug.

"Bowser knows I'm right," he said.

"Time will tell," Norman said gloomily as he climbed into Alfie's pocket. "I'm going to catch up on my sleep. Night, all."

Adeline blew down Alfie's neck. "Let's hope for the

best, dear boy. In the meantime, if you'll excuse me, I'm going to have a little graze."

"Why don't you have a sleep as well, Alfie?" Penelope suggested. "I'll keep watch. I think you're right – Bilinda will come back – but however fast she walks she's unlikely to be here for quite a while."

Alfie nodded. "Thanks," he said, and seconds later he was fast asleep.

Chapter Nineteen

THE HOURS WENT SLOWLY BY. Perce popped down
a couple of times to report that Flugg was chewing
a bone while Grindbone paced up and down waiting
for the next prince to arrive. When Alfie woke and
saw how far the sun had moved across the sky, he sat
up with a jump. "How long have I slept?" he asked
anxiously.

"Not long, darling," Penelope soothed. "Bilinda had
to get back to her house, unlock the cage and let out
all the princes, remember. And find those bottles of –
was it snail potion?"

"Poppy snail soup," Alfie said. He got to his feet

and stared up at the castle. He could see Perce on top of one of the flagpoles, but was he still keeping watch? He wasn't moving. Alfie squinched his eyes and looked again. He was almost sure Perce had his head under his wing. Picking up a small pebble, Alfie threw it at the castle wall, but he couldn't throw high enough to wake the sleeping bird.

"**What what what's going on?**" Bowser was sitting up, tail wagging.

"I think Perce is asleep," Alfie said. "And anything might be happening on the other side of the castle. But I can't call him. The ogres would hear me!"

Bowser pointed his nose at Alfie's back pocket. "**Yurt Yurt Yurt,**" he said.

"What about Yurt?" Mystified, Alfie put his hand in his pocket – and pulled out the catapult his brother had given him.

"Bowser! You're a genius!"

Fitting a small stone to the catapult, he took careful aim at the tower below the flagpole. The stone flew up in a graceful arc and rattled against the wall. Perce woke with a start, looked wildly round, then froze … and Alfie knew he'd seen something unexpected. His heart began to race. Was it Bilinda and Magnifico? Or something much worse?

The magpie was flying now, circling over the castle … and yes! He was headed towards Alfie. "Prince on approach!" he squawked. "Prince on approach!"

Alfie stared. "A prince? Coming here?"

"Riding to the castle. Big white horse, sparkly crown – VERY sparkly crown. It's a proper prince!"

"How far away is he?" Alfie asked.

"I'll go and see." And Perce flew off again, leaving Alfie rubbing his nose as he wondered what to do.

"I'll have to warn the prince about the ogres," he decided, and he looked at Adeline.

"Would you mind giving me a ride?"

"My pleasure, dear boy," the horse said.

As Alfie hurried towards her, there was another flurry of black and white. For a moment Alfie thought it was Perce again, but it was Kev – Kev looking bright of eye and delighted with his news. "Hero and companion five minutes away," he reported. "So you'd best nip round to the front of the castle. Careful how you go – the big ogre's not happy. He's muttering and stamping and looking as black as thunder."

It took Alfie a moment to take in what Kev was saying; it was Penelope who asked, "So Bilinda came back with Magnifico? Has she got the sleeping potion?"

Kev winked. "You should see what she's brought back! There's bags of gold! But yes, a bottle too. Strong stuff, that. She had to drag those princes out into the forest before they could even stand … and did they thank her? Not a bit of it. Scarpered as soon as their legs stopped wobbling. No manners. No manners at all. Now, are we on the move? Chop chop! No time to waste!"

"But there's another prince coming," Alfie said. "I need to warn him!"

"If you ask me, you should let him come." Norman had reappeared on Alfie's shoulder and was cleaning his whiskers. "The prince arrives, the ogres bop him on the head, they carry him away – and Bob's your uncle! You've got a clear run at the castle and the princess!"

"I can't let that happen." Alfie shook his head. "No … either we warn the prince, or we try the sleeping potion on the ogres."

"I'd go for the potion," Kev advised. "It'll take you ages to reach the prince. Besides, what if he doesn't believe you?"

Alfie made up his mind. "The potion it is!"

The party tiptoed back round the castle, Bowser once more leading the way. His ears were pricked for any unusual sounds, and twice he stopped to listen. Alfie, uncomfortably aware of his heart thumping, grew more and more nervous. When they finally crept through the bracken and he saw Bilinda sitting by the hollow tree, he gave a huge sigh of relief. The birdcage was by her side; the perch had gone, and been

replaced by cushions
... and Magnifico was
lolling back licking
crumbs off his fingers.

"Maggers!" Alfie said,
and he rushed forward.
"Bilinda! I'm so
pleased to see you!"

The ogre smiled at him, but his brother did not. "Huh! I hope you've enjoyed lazing around here, Alfie, while we did all the work." He gave a dramatic sigh. "Well, I suppose that's what a hero has to do. Let six princes out of prison. Collect bottles of extremely nasty soup. Pack up loads of gold ... and very heavy it was, too."

"Oh, chubbly wubbly!" Bilinda gave him a fond smile. "Is all for my precious chubbly wubbly!"

Magnifico waved a lordly hand. "If you say so. Is there any more of that cake? Or a bun?"

Bilinda leant into the hollow tree and pulled out a bag. She gave Magnifico a large iced bun, then brought

out an evil-looking dark green bottle.
"Here sleepy poppy snail soup."

"Thanks." Alfie took the bottle
cautiously, remembering the
effect it had had on the princes.
"They don't need to drink it, do they?
We can just crack it open somewhere nearby."

"Best on heads," Bilinda said. "Drop on heads,
sleep DEEP!"

"So … won't it work otherwise?" Alfie asked.

The ogre girl looked doubtful. "Maybe little, little
sleep. Ogres strong!"

The bottle was heavy, and Alfie swung it carefully
to and fro, feeling its weight. How could he drop it on
the ogres' heads? If he could get to the top of the tower
it would be easy – but that was impossible. And it was
much too heavy for Kev and Perce to carry, even had
he been able to invent some kind of sling to put it in.
Could he throw it?

Bilinda was watching him. "I can throw," she said.
"Bilinda very strong!"

"Really?" Alfie's hopes rose again. "You can throw that high?"

There was a sudden interruption. "Akakakakak!" Kev was looking flustered. "Watch it! The ogre must have heard something ... he's sniffing around and he's coming this way – and Flugg's coming too!"

"NOOOOOOOOOOOOOOOOOOOOOOOOOO!"

Magnifico's scream of terror echoed throughout the forest. Immediately Bilinda stood up. With one hand she thrust the hero's cage into a hollow tree, and with the other she grasped the bottle. "Bilinda HATE Dadda!" she muttered, and she looked at Alfie. "Bilinda throw bottle."

"Just a minute!" Alfie was kneeling on the path, frantically looking for stones. If the sleeping potion was to drop on both ogres, the bottle had to be broken in mid-air – and he could only think of one way to do it. The catapult was in his hand ... and yes! There was the perfect stone. The sound of heavy bodies crashing through the undergrowth was getting nearer and nearer, and he could already hear heavy breathing.

"Ready!" he said, although his hands were shaking. "I'm ready, Bilinda!"

"One – three – five – THROW!" Bilinda bellowed, and the bottle soared up into the air.

Alfie drew back the elastic on his catapult, and squinted upwards. "Here goes!"

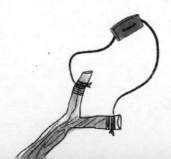

Chapter Twenty

IF BILINDA HADN'T SHOUTED, the potion would have missed its target. Hearing her, Grindbone and Flugg stopped – and at that exact moment Alfie's stone hit the bottle flying over their heads. The CRACK! made them look up just as the torrent of grey-greenish slime poured down, covering their heads and shoulders and filling the air with a sickly sweet smell that made Alfie's eyes stream and his throat ache.

"AAAAAAAAAAAAGH!" bellowed Grindbone, and he thrashed his club wildly from side to side.

"AAAAAAAAAAAAGH!" echoed Flugg, and he sank to his knees.

"AAAAAAAaaaaghhh…" The large ogre's roar grew fainter and fainter, gradually fading into gentle moaning. The moaning became a sigh and, finally, the sigh became a loud and purposeful snore. A moment later it was joined by a second snore, quieter, but just as steady.

"Is sleep," Bilinda remarked. She hauled the hero's cage out of the tree, and opened the door. "There, little chubbly wubbly, Bilinda's precious ickle pickle is safe. Go find your princess."

"Really?" Magnifico looked nervously round.

"Yes. Is all safe." The ogre's voice shook a little as she helped him out. "And … and pretty princess is waiting. Bilinda wishes you good luck." She heaved an enormous sigh.

Magnifico stood on the forest floor, a half-eaten bun in one hand, a biscuit in the other. "Alfie, are you ready? Your hero is waiting for you!"

Alfie didn't answer. He was looking anxiously at Penelope, who was collapsed on Adeline's saddle, fast asleep … or was she? Her breathing was very shallow.

"I'll take her a little further away, dear boy," Adeline said, and sneezed. "That's powerful stuff! But fresh air should do the trick. How's Norman?"

Norman was lying in Alfie's pocket, as limp as his sister. Alfie placed him carefully beside Penelope, coughing as he did so.

"Small lungs," Adeline explained. "They'll pick up, no worries. But I suggest you give those ogres a wide berth. There's green smoke hanging in the air, and we don't want you and the hero dozing off."

"**Woof! Other way way way!**" Bowser agreed.

It was good advice, and Alfie took it. He led Magnifico away from the ogres as Bowser walked briskly in front, wagging his tail importantly.

"Hey, Maggers!" Alfie gave his brother's arm a cheerful shake. "Guess what! You're on your way to kiss a princess … and find your Happily Ever After!"

"H'mph." The hero sounded less than enthusiastic. "I hope she's worth the trouble. AND she's got lots and lots of gold. AND she's good at cooking." He licked the last of the icing off the bun he was holding. "Bilinda's a very good cook."

"Aren't you excited?" Alfie asked. "I am!"

"You haven't got boots that pinch your toes," Magnifico said. "I was in absolute agony until I was carried." He gave Alfie a sharp look. "I hope you're not expecting me to climb any stairs."

"I think there might be stairs," Alfie said – and then he and Magnifico were out from the sheltering trees and walking towards the castle. And there, standing in front of them, was a snow-white horse.

Its saddle and bridle were gold, hung with tinkling bells, and the rider was just as glorious. He was dressed in scarlet velvet from head to foot, there was a crown on his head, and he was holding a lute.

"It's a prince!" Alfie whispered. "He's ever so grand."

As he and Magnifico came closer, hardly able to believe what was in front of them, the prince began to sing. *"Oh lady fair, with golden hair, I come to sing you this – I've travelled far, but here I are, to wake you with a kiss…"* He frowned. "No no. That's not at all right." Alfie coughed, and the prince dropped his lute in surprise. As Alfie ran to pick it up, he backed his horse away. "I say, are you a troll?"

"No," Alfie said. "I'm a boy. I'm Alfie Onion, and this is my brother Magnifico."

Magnifico, flakes of dried slime clinging to his hair and clothes, puffed out his chest. "That's me! I'm the seventh son of a seventh son. I'm a hero!"

"Really?" The prince raised his eyebrows. "That's so amazing! I'm the seventh son of a seventh son too! Actually – I don't suppose you've seen any of my brothers, have you? They've been gone for ages, and Mummy and Daddy are terribly worried. They went off one by one to kiss the princess, you see. When Jules didn't come back, Boodles went to look for him – and kiss the princess of course. And then Boodles didn't come back either, so Rufus went looking … and now all six are missing, so there's only me left. Grandioso, seventh son of King Septimus. Poor Mummy's beside herself!"

"They were caught by the ogres, Grindbone and Flugg," Alfie said. "And they were put in a cage."

"But I set them free." Magnifico puffed out his chest a little more. "That's what a hero does, you know. They were in a cage, but Bilin— I mean, I opened the locks and let them out."

"Oh, I say, how terribly kind of you." The prince took the lute from Alfie, and swung himself off his horse. "I suppose they've wandered off home? Haw haw haw! They'll probably be back before I am." He moved towards Alfie and the hero, then changed his mind. "I say, have you chaps had an accident or something? If you don't mind my saying so, you do whiff rather."

"We fell in the ogre's rubbish pit. But I escaped," Magnifico boasted.

"I SAY! You're a real hero, aren't you?" The prince seemed genuinely impressed. "Are you going to have a shot at waking the princess? Kiss her, and all that?"

"That's what I'm here for." Magnifico nodded. "I'm going to kiss the princess, and live Happily Ever After in Glorious Luxury."

"Haw haw haw!" The prince laughed again. "You're a splendid chap! Must remember to tell old Jules that one. Glorious Luxury, eh? What'll you do with the bats and rats and spiders?"

Magnifico went pale. "Bats? Rats? Spiders?"

"I say, didn't you know? This old dump's been more or less empty for years." The prince was walking up the castle steps as he spoke, and he twisted the iron handle on the door. There was a creak as the door swung open, and Alfie gasped. In front of him was a huge hall that must once have been fine – but was now draped with cobwebs and thick with dust. There was no furniture apart from a couple of broken chairs, and no sign of human life.

"See?" The prince waved a hand. "It's been like this for ever."

Alfie looked at him in surprise. "Have you been here before?"

"Not me." Grandioso shook his head. "But when Daddy was a boy he managed to cut down enough roses to reach a window and climb in. Didn't manage to wake the princess, though. The windows have all been shuttered since then."

"But … but why didn't the princess wake up?" A terrible thought came to Alfie. "There IS a princess, isn't there?"

"Oh yes." The prince nodded. "Daddy says she's poor as a church mouse. Not so much as a silver cup in her room." Grandioso put his finger to his nose and winked. "Tell you a secret. Don't think Daddy even tried to kiss her when he saw her! But you never know. Today might be your lucky day."

Magnifico was drooping more and more. "Poor as a church mouse? And a crumbling castle. What's the point?"

"Come on, Magnifico," Alfie said encouragingly. "This is what we've come for! The journey, dealing with the ogres – it'll all be wasted if you don't climb those stairs."

Grandioso was shuffling his feet. "Actually, why don't you have first go? Rather hoping she doesn't wake up for me, if I'm honest. Got a gal back home – Princess Alice. Lovely, lovely gal. Don't know what I'd do if this one woke up. Alice wouldn't be pleased. Not at all."

"So why are you even trying?" Alfie asked.

Grandioso looked astonished. "It's what princes have to do! Part of our training. Find a castle, cut down the roses, kiss a princess … don't you heroes do it too?"

"I'm not a hero," Alfie said. "But I promised Ma that Maggers would do everything a hero does in the fairy tales."

"Better get on with it then," the prince said. "After you!"

Chapter Twenty-One

It was a very long way to the top of the castle tower, and Magnifico complained at every step. When they finally reached a small wooden door and could go no further, he sank down with a loud groan. "This had better be worth it," he said. "Open the door, Alfie. I'm not up to it."

The door was stiff, but Alfie noticed there were no cobwebs and the hinges were oiled. *Strange*, he thought. *Very strange*. Then the handle turned, and he found himself in a small whitewashed room with a bare wooden floor and a plain iron bedstead in the corner. The covers were spotlessly white, and so was the pillow … and lying in the bed, sleeping soundly, was a girl with tumbling brown curls.

"Huh!" Magnifico had followed Alfie in. "I thought that mouse said she was pretty."

"She is," Alfie said. He was gazing at the princess, and something curious was happening inside him. His heart was fluttering, and his legs had turned to jelly. "She's very pretty. Very pretty indeed…"

"She's got a snub nose," Magnifico said.

"She's plain." Grandioso had joined them. "Not like my beautiful Alice. Are you going to kiss her?"

"I suppose so." Magnifico bent down and gave the princess a quick peck. She didn't stir ... but Alfie, who was looking intently at her face, wondered if he had imagined a faint twitch of her nose.

"There!" Magnifico stood back. "She hasn't woken up. What do we do now?"

"Shall I have a try?" Grandioso stepped forward. "I've had a wheeze of an idea! If she wakes up for me – after all, I AM a prince as well as the seventh son of a seventh son – you can have her!"

"Ah." The hero considered this. "I suppose that might do. But would I get the castle? And the gold? If there is any, that is."

"Everything!" The prince put his hand to his heart. "I don't need a penny."

"OK, then." Magnifico stood back. "You try."

The prince swept a magnificent bow, then knelt beside the bed. "Wake, lovely princess, wake!"

Nothing happened.

"Phew!" Grandioso sounded profoundly relieved. Alfie, who had been holding his breath, was just as pleased. She might have a snub nose, but to him the princess looked perfect. He would have been horrified if she'd woken up for either Magnifico or Prince Grandioso. She deserved much, much better.

"I'll be off, then." Magnifico was already limping to the door. "There's nothing here – nothing at all. I don't like this castle. It's rubbish. I never want to live somewhere like this! And there's no gold…" He turned to give Alfie a frosty glare. "Do you know what? I'm going home to Pigsticking Farm, and I'm going to take Bilinda with me. I never did want to be a hero. It was all Ma's idea … she wanted me to do all the work so she could live in Glorious Luxury. Well, I'll tell you something. Bilinda's bags are full of gold – FULL of it! And it's all for me! So I'm going to live like a king! And Bilinda's going to cook me pies and puddings, and we'll live Happily Ever After!" He paused in the doorway. "I'll see you back at the farm, Alfie Onion. And don't think I'm going to say you helped me. You were no help at all. Now, I'm going to slide down the stairs on my bottom. My boots are killing me…"

"I say, wait for me." Grandioso was in just as much of a hurry. "Race you to the door!"

And they were gone.

Alfie sighed. What would his mother say? Would she be horribly disappointed? He was afraid she would be. He gave the princess one last lingering look, and turned away.

"Boy? Come back! It's your turn!" Startled, Alfie swung round. The princess was sitting up and smiling at him. "Hurry up! Come and kiss me!"

Hardly daring to believe his ears and eyes, Alfie walked slowly towards the bed. The princess lay back on her pillow and closed her eyes – and looked exactly as if she was deep in an enchanted sleep.

"Here goes," Alfie said to himself. He took a deep breath, and kissed the princess.

It was as if the sun had suddenly burst through the ceiling. The little room was filled with colour, and the bed was heaped with velvet and silk and satin. The carpet was so thick and rich that Alfie's feet sank deep in it, and damask curtains sprigged with pink and silver flowers hung at the windows.

"Wow!" Alfie said. "WOW!"

In a moment the princess was on her feet, and laughing. "At last!" she said. "At last! I've been waiting ages and ages and AGES for someone like you!" She made a face. "You see, I woke up after the hundred years all by myself … so after that, I had to pretend to be asleep. All those dreary princes – yuck! But the moment I saw you from my window I just knew you were the one!" She giggled. "I used to peep out between the shutters to see who was there. Ooof! Those horrible ogres! They gave me goose-pimples! Come on—" she seized Alfie's hand— "Hurry up, we've got to go and tell Mother and Father!"

Alfie hesitated. "Your mother and father? Are they far away?"

"They're downstairs, silly!" The princess laughed again. "Oh! This is ridiculous! I don't even know your name."

"Erm … Alfie," Alfie said, suddenly shy. "Alfie Onion."

"So I'll be Princess Mary Onion?" This time the princess had to sit down, she was laughing so much. "Oh, I love it! And I love you, Alfie Onion!"

"Mary," Alfie said thoughtfully. "That's a lovely name." A blush swept from the roots of his hair to the tips of his toes. "And…" he swallowed hard, unable to speak.

"Go on," Mary encouraged. "Go on, Alfie Onion!"

Alfie looked into her big brown eyes. "I love you too!"

"Good," Mary said. "It would be a terrible disappointment to me if you didn't. Heroes always fall in love with the princess at first glance, you know."

"But I'm not a hero," Alfie said. "I'm—"

"A hero," Mary said firmly. "Who got rid of the ogres? You did. I saw you!"

"The ogres!" Alfie had forgotten about them. At some point they were sure to wake up … and what then? Would they attack the castle? "We need to get away from here," he said urgently. "The ogres – they're dangerous!"

Mary was throwing back the shutters at one of the staircase windows. "I don't think you need worry," she said. "Come and see."

Alfie came to stand beside her, and the two of them looked out over the forest. From high up in the tower they could see the ogres clearly … but what was happening to them? Hundreds of trolls were busying themselves about the fallen figures with ropes and levers. As Alfie and Mary watched, the ogres were bundled unceremoniously onto a rough cart pulled by ten of the biggest trolls, and a moment later they were being trundled away to the sound of wildly enthusiastic trollish cheering.

"Where are they taking them?" Alfie wondered.

The princess shrugged. "Who knows? Far, far away. They won't ever come back. They've been defeated – they'll be too ashamed."

Alfie was craning his neck to see what else was going on down below. "There's Rootlie Toot. And there's the little troll who talked to me when I was in the tree. Look! Down by Grindbone's toes."

"That's Nubbins," Mary said. "I used to play with him when I was little." She waved, and called, "Cooeeee! Nubbins, I can see you!"

The troll looked up, and a wide grin spread across his face. "Princess find magic hero humbly body! Am thanking magic hero very greatly. Did tricksie ogres. Now us trolls have peace."

Mary gave a final wave, then turned to Alfie. "So – are you ready to meet Mother and Father?"

"Oh…" Alfie looked down at his filthy clothes. "I don't think they'll like the look of me much."

"Rubbish," Mary said. "It doesn't matter what you look like. That's why the enchantment made everything look so old and dirty and dusty. If people like your

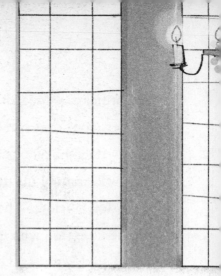

brother knew what the castle was really like, they'd be pounding on the door every second minute. Come and see." She giggled again. "It's pretty impressive!"

Mary was right. When she and Alfie reached the great hall, Alfie stood spellbound in the doorway, quite unable to take it all in. There were wonderful tapestries covering the walls, glittering chandeliers hung above a long table piled high with golden plates and silver cups, and all around were chairs covered in the softest velvet. Servants were gliding to and fro, but as Mary pulled Alfie forward they stepped to one side and bowed and curtsied.

"It's *you* they're curtseying to," Mary whispered. "You're the hero who's rescued us!"

Alfie couldn't answer. At the end of the hall were

two high thrones, and sitting on them were a king and
a queen, wearing royal robes of red and gold. Mary
tugged at his arm. "They won't hurt you, Alfie. Look
how they're smiling! They're thrilled to bits!"

She was right. The queen had jumped to her feet
and was running to meet them. She threw her arms
first round Mary, then Alfie, while the king patted
Alfie's back over and over again muttering, "Splendid!
Thank you, old chap! Thank you so much! Splendid!
Splendid!"

"Mother, Father," Mary said. "this is Alfie Onion. We're going to be married – isn't it fun?"

"Darlings!" the queen said. "Come and sit down … and Alfie, tell me all about yourself." She gave her daughter a loving kiss. "It's so good to see you so happy." Mary kissed her mother back. "I'm happier than I've ever been!" She pirouetted across the hall. "Alfie – can we go outside? I haven't been outside for a hundred years!"

A moment later the two of them were hurrying out through the castle door. As they did so, a row of heralds dressed in scarlet and silver played a trumpet fanfare, and Alfie shook his head in wonder.

"It's just like a fairy tale. It really is! Mary, would it be all right to bring my mother here, do you think? It's what she's always dreamed of…"

"Of course it'd be all right! She can come and live here any time.

There's a whole wing of the castle that's empty – she can have that." Mary blew Alfie a kiss. "But we can live wherever we want, Alfie dearest. We can run over the hills and far away … wherever we are, we'll live Happily Ever After for certain sure."

"For certain sure," Alfie agreed. "We'll live Happily Ever After."

Chapter Twenty-Two

AND ALFIE ONION and Princess Mary Onion did
live Happily Ever After. Mary was delighted to meet
Penelope and Norman, and suggested that they
might like to live in the castle rather than beside
it. This pleased Penelope very much, but Norman
complained that he missed the fresh air. Adeline
settled happily into the royal stables, and waited
hopefully for the first royal baby to arrive. Bowser
took to royal life with enthusiasm; the bones were
the biggest he'd ever seen, and he adored Princess
Mary. Kev and Perce were rewarded with a whole
heap of twinkly sparkly shiny stuff, and Perce had

a warm hen's egg every Thursday for breakfast.

Happiest of all was Aggie Onion. She spent half the year at Pigsticking Farm – Garf Onion refused to leave his pigs, and Princess Mary refused to build a royal pigsty beside the castle – and the other half in Rosewall Castle enjoying Glorious Luxury. It had taken her a little while to adjust to having an exceptionally large ogre as a daughter-in-law, but Bilinda worked so hard, and was so very strong, that Aggie had nothing to do all day except paint her toenails and curl her hair. Magnifico had done well for himself, Aggie told her neighbours. Surprisingly well, all things considered. But nobody had done as well as her darling son, Alfie. Alfie, Aggie said, was her hero.

And Aggie also was waiting hopefully for the first royal baby. She had a book to read to him or her…

A book of fairy tales.

Also by Vivian French
TALES FROM THE FIVE KINGDOMS

"24-carat gold. I forgot reading could be this much fun!"
Philip Ardagh

"Hilarious adventures with wicked witches, trolls, bats and fairy-tale magic." *Books for Keeps*

"Delightfully witty and exciting."
Independent on Sunday

"Fabulous." *Daily Telegraph*

"So good, I was up all night reading. But don't tell my mum!"
Grace, aged 11½

Vivian French

lives in Edinburgh, and writes in a messy workroom
stuffed full of fairy tales and folk tales — the stories she
loves best. She's brilliant at retelling classic tales, as she did
for *The Most Wonderful Thing in the World*, and has created
worlds of her own in the Tales From the Five Kingdoms and
the Tiara Club series. Vivian teaches at Edinburgh College
of Art and can be seen at festivals all over the country.
She is one of the most borrowed children's authors in UK
libraries, and in 2016 was awarded the MBE for services
to literature, literacy, illustration and the arts.

Marta Kissi

is an exciting new talent in the world of children's book
illustration. Originally from Warsaw, she came to Britain
to study Illustration and Animation at Kingston University,
and then Art and Design at the Royal College of Art. Her
favourite part of being an illustrator is bringing stories to
life by designing charming characters and the wonderful
worlds they live in. Marta shares a studio in London with
her boyfriend and their pet plant Trevor.